Entombed in Glass

Unfortunate Soul Chronicles
Book Two

Stacey Rourke

Torn from all that truly mattered;
a hero defined, a soul shattered.

CHAPTER ONE

Mirror, mirror on the wall.
You've all heard that fated call.
To the seer of present, future, and past,
a nameless face entombed in glass.
I know all,
I see all,
I can answer all ... with flair.
Though to tell you the truth, I really don't care.
Matters of mortals? Surely, you jest?
With no solid form, I find their troubles a yawn fest.
I guess I should mention I don't have to rhyme.
Stuck in this wasteland, it passes the time.
Without such tricks and distractions, my mind would be
destroyed,
lost and ravaged by this endless void.
If ending it all were an option, I would have done it by now.
Unfortunately, with no solid stature, I can't fathom how.

ROURKE

Instead, I focus on those that cursed me here,
formidable connivers that many fear.
I do their bidding as a trusted pawn,
yet claims of my loyalty couldn't be more wrong.
Each day that passes I scheme to break free from their thrall,
to honor a self-made vow ... and kill them all.

CHAPTER TWO

The stench of charred flesh gagged me. A cloud of smoke and rubble burned my eyes and scorched down my throat. Through that cloud of misery, *she* called to me. Her muffled siren song lured me back from the teetering edge of the beyond.

Coming to under a pile of rocks, I discovered blackened bones littered my chest. Gingerly brushing them aside, I forced myself up to sitting. Nausea caused the world to whirl around me, its force pounding spikes into my skull. Dabbing two fingers at the tender pressure point at my temple, I pulled them back to find blots of blood smearing my skin. What hit me, I couldn't say. Regardless, that wasn't to blame for the bile bubbling up the back of my throat.

I was sitting in a nest of bodies.

Death's violent hold marred the terrain as far as the eye could see. Mermen and humans alike slaughtered and left for dead without an ounce of mercy.

Only then did my hazy mind manage to form the memories of what had come to pass. Princess Vanessa of Atlantica, for whom I had joined the Royal Guard to be worthy of, evoked a spell to grant us mer-soldiers legs. Her goal? Allowing us the opportunity to, quite literally, gain ground in our war against the humans of

3

Lemuria. Vanessa's bold maneuver worked—for a time. Evidence of that laid in the Lemuria castle now crumbling into the sea. What fleeting victory we claimed was brutally stolen by the horror that followed. Without warning, Vanessa's spell … broke. Mermen screamed in anguish as they were robbed of their borrowed legs. Collapsing to the ground in vulnerable heaps, their tails returned. From there, the Lemuria soldiers killed them with ease. Stabbing bayonets into their flipping fins, they left many to slow, torturous deaths. Others were given the quick release of a blade's edge.

I should have been one of them.

That was my place, among my men.

I could vividly recall the clap of my sword against that of a foul-breathed human's. As I gained the upper hand in my push against him, magic swirled around me. Light reflected off the hint of my sunset orange scales returning.

Then … nothing.

I had no recollection of how it was I maintained the soot-covered legs stretched out before me, as so many others were cheated of theirs.

It had to be Vanessa. Somehow … she saved me.

Surrounded by ghastly misery, her noble act of kindness seemed tragically unjust. How did I rate, in the scheme of things, to draw breath while flies buzzed around the corpses of my fellow soldiers?

"*Alllllllastor.*" So lost was I in my own reverie, that I almost missed the call of my name riding in on a lashing breeze. It was the familiar lilt of the voice that launched my heart into a hammering crescendo, and snapped my head around.

As I struggled to lift my crumpled form from the ground, the rocks beneath me gouged my palms. Finding footing, I tried to rise on unsteady legs.

"*Vanessa!*" The left limb held. The right crumbled like dried seaweed under my weight. Treacherous knee buckling, it forced a pained yelp through my gritted teeth when it connected with the earth. White-hot pain roared through my thigh. Hand trembling, I reached down to gingerly touch a wound I didn't know I had. Neck craned, I cringed at the slice tore in the back of my leg. The muscle was filleted, tissue and tendon hanging slack in a gruesome cavity.

"*Allllaaastor!*" Vanessa's voice—or perhaps my mind's mocking illusion of it—called a second time. She sounded farther away. Like a lifeboat sailing on in search of survivors, every moment I hesitated, the opportunity drifted farther from reach.

Desperation seeped through my veins, urging me into motion. Cracked and bleeding hands clawing at the blood-soaked earth, I dragged myself over the devastation with one working leg. I couldn't allow myself to think of the forms beneath me as *actual* beings. Not yet. Such thoughts would render me immobile. Instead, with the acrid taste of ash burned onto my tongue, I focused every ounce of my remaining strength on reaching the peak in the landscape up ahead.

Sweating and straining, I forced my elbows and forearms to guide me up the terrain when my battered hands could take no more. What could have been a second, or an eternity later, I crested that lofty summit.

Heart skipping like a dolphin riding waves, I caught a glimpse of her. Vanessa, my angel of mercy, crouched down to speak to another survivor—concern creasing her brow, strands of raven hair lashing at her pink cheeks.

Even at that distance, I recognized her patient with equal parts awe and bewilderment. Of all the dedicated, able-bodied members of the Royal Guard, *Sterling* was the absolute last person I expected to see alive. Once, he occupied the cell opposite Vanessa's when she was wrongfully imprisoned in the dungeon of Atlantica's castle. The penance for *his* crimes had been a forced position on the front line of the war. Hers … was a disgusting display it made my blood boil to think of. But that's her story to tell.

Mine involves the day Sterling was assigned to my platoon, and I watched his bumbling antics, full of doubt he could make it three steps on land. That was in large part due to his ramblings about a pipe-puffing caterpillar, and something called a Jabberwock. But, I digress. Despite my skepticisms, he survived. I gladly accepted this blessing from Mother Ocean, and allowed the eccentric lad to bend Vanessa's ear long enough for me to heave myself within shouting distance.

Sweat dripping from my brow, I shuffled on. Dead, unseeing eyes assaulted me from all sides. Broken, discarded weapons scraped at my flesh. Still, I lurched on.

Between the breaking waves, the wind tossed a few random words of their conversation back at me.

"… only needed to get to the water."

"Common sense …"

"Alastor … gone?"

Swiping at her cheeks with the back of her hand, Vanessa brushed away tears that slipped from her lashes.

Making no attempts to comfort her, Sterling drummed one finger against his bottom lip. "… ever really here at all?"

Snapping upright, Vanessa shouted words that were swallowed by the ocean's thunder.

The quirky little man merely cocked his head in response.

Shoulders sagging, her gaze drifted to the sea.

A fist of fear closed around my throat. In moments, I would lose her. Biting back the pain, I forced myself up on my good leg. Limping onward, I reached for her, shouting her name loud enough to make my lungs ache.

Mother Ocean, let her look up. Let her see me.

The mercy I pleaded for was lost to the ocean's roar. Pulse drumming against my ribs, I hauled myself onward. Every muscle in my body ached. The shroud of defeat set in as her amethyst stare locked on the horizon.

"*Vanessa!*" I tried again, throat raw from emotion.

Cawing seagulls swooped overhead, drowning out my raspy shout.

In reluctant acceptance, Vanessa took a step toward the shoreline. Then another. Each squish of sand beneath her toes stomped my heart to shards.

"*Vanessa!*" Every ounce of my being pleaded for her chin to tip my way. One sweeping glance could secure our forever. Acting on reckless abandon, I damned the pain and heaved myself onward. Afraid tearing my gaze away would mean losing her, I didn't glance down at the debris blocking my path until my foot caught on the cold, clammy tail of a fallen merman. A fresh blaze of anguish scorched through my leg, slamming me down on the bed of rock and carnage.

Blood gushed down the back of my thigh in a steady stream, the world spinning around me in a dizzying blur. Planting my palms, I pushed myself up in time to see the gleam of Vanessa's violet fins dive to the depths.

Her name tore from my chest in a final plea she would never hear.

My future ... my forever ... disappeared beneath the cresting waves.

With nothing left to cling to, my head and hopes crumpled into the sand.

CHAPTER THREE

he seemed sweet. You *really* should have stopped her," a husky voice pointed out, the shadow of the newcomer stretching over my crumpled form.

Vision blurring, I blinked hard to focus my gaze warped by blood loss. A current of raven hair, tinged with hints of blue, framed broad shoulders. The sharp angles of his bone structure reminded me of the unforgiving features of the Artic merfolk. His modest grey robe was tattered and singed along the bottom hem, it's frayed fabric swaying around his ankles like licking black flames.

"Royal Alchemist Hades?" I croaked, bowing my head out of equal parts respect and blood loss. I was just a boy when he and his brother, Poseidon, petitioned Mount Olympus to have him reallocated from Atlantica. Even so, I could vividly recall being in awe of the power that crackled from him like a brewing storm.

"Now, now," Hades confirmed his identity with a dismissive wave of his hand, "that's not necessary."

Dutifully, I dragged myself up onto one knee. Injured leg stretched out uncooperatively behind me, I clamped one shaky fist over my heart. "You are royalty, Your Highness. As a member of the Royal Guard, it is my duty and privilege to honor you by addressing you as such."

Hades' face fell slack of emotion, his lip curling with a hint of distaste. "Quaint, but not what I meant. I'm a Lord now. You're not supposed to make eye contact, or speak in my presence." Face an impassive neutral, he blinked my way for a beat before a charming smile coiled at the corner of his lips. "I'm kidding, of course. I mean, I *am* a Lord, but most of my subjects take the no talking thing to an extreme. Therefore, I *welcome* that faux pas."

"I'm sure they only mean that as a show of respect, my Lord." Keeping my head ducked, I grit my teeth as the throbbing in my thigh triggered black spots that swam before my eyes.

"Quite the contrary, they're all dead."

Brow pinched tight, my posture swayed as I glanced up.

Eyes crinkling with amusement at my confusion, Hades chuckled. "My title is as Lord of the Underworld. The moans from the River Styx are the closest I get to conversation most days."

Shifting my crumpled leg beneath me, I cleared my throat to mask the blinding bolts of pain jolting through my torso. "What … is such a regal man doing in a damned place such as this?"

"Life takes us—" Hades' calm colloquy cut off, bubbling panic widening his eyes. Mouth gaping, his cheeks contracted in frantic gulps. Managing to choke out a labored croak, he swallowed hard in victory over the momentarily crippling onslaught. "My apologies. When Zeus granted me human form he left in the part of my brain that thinks I'm supposed to be breathing water. Every now and then, my body believes it is suffocating. Nothing more fun than sporadically thinking you're dying. But, enough about me. Tell me about your little mermaid. Risqué falling for a princess, isn't it? How tragically taboo."

Knowing my place in the hierarchy, my only choice was to deny my love, no matter how it pained me. "No, m'lord. I sought only her guidance to deliver me back home."

Fiddling with the crystal charm strung around his neck, Hades screwed his thin lips to the side, his stare fixed on the lapping waves. "Yes, of course. I always sob uncontrollably when I need directions. Tell me, is it a habit of yours to lie to royals, or is this a new—albeit it, dangerous—hobby you're sampling?"

Sagging forward, I caught myself with one hand. Choking on pain, I managed a grunted response. "A thousand apologies, m'lord. I know any feelings I may, or may not, have for the princess, *your niece,* are strictly forbidden. I meant no disrespect."

Hades bristled, his chin lifting with a haughty twitch. "I cannot, and will not, fault *anyone* for falling in love. That euphoric agony is one that enslaves us and drives us to madness or salvation. I could wax poetic on the topic until the sun sets over the waters' edge. However, I feel I should first point out that you're bleeding in torrents."

"Huh," I mused, fading onto my elbows. Slurred speech tumbled from my thick tongue in a mess of consonants. "That would explain why you're getting all blurry."

Dragging one heel back, Hades shifted his weight to face me. "It would be my humble pleasure to help. But I'm afraid I have to ask for one small favor in return."

Unable to hold up my own weight, I slumped to the ground. "Name your terms," I mumbled, darkness seeping in from all sides.

The crystal around his neck pulsing with a hypnotic sapphire luminescence, Hades crouched beside me to whisper against my ear. "You are a soldier, driven by honor before all else. Are you not?"

Fading fast, I forced my heavy lids to blink to stop my eyes from rolling back. "Yes, m'lord."

With the side of his knuckle under my chin, Hades lifted my head and caught my wavering stare. "I know your kind. You believe that by doing what's right, the gods of fate will reward in turn. I call upon this sense of honor, now. Pledge yourself to me. In exchange, I *will* help you."

Something in his words sent icy fingers prickling up my spine. "I pledged an oath of fealty to King Triton, Ruler of Atlantica. I serve his majesty."

Expelling a disappointed sigh, Hades released me and drew himself up to full height. "I really hoped you wouldn't say that." Stalking a slow circle around me, he smoothed the front of his threadbare robe. "You see, *King Triton* is the reason you're lying there right now. Had he not forced his agenda upon Vanessa, she would have had time to perfect her spell. It was his pride, and fear of losing that coveted throne, which prevented him from granting her that." Pausing next to my hip, he stomped one sandaled foot down on my oozing wound.

Cannon blasts of anguish tore a scream from my core.

"Triton's only power is in his title. You know that, as well as I do. Do you believe your *finned king*," he spat the words as if they soured on his tongue, "could help you now?"

Forehead falling to the crook of my arm, my lip curled from my teeth as images of a young Triton wrestling with baby manatees played through my mind. "No, he couldn't. But ... it doesn't matter. I stooped before him and made my vow."

Removing his foot, Hades edged back a step. Head tilted, he considered me with wry amusement. Making the most of the momentary liberation, I rolled to my side and filled my lungs with greedy gulps of air.

"I appreciate your valor. I do. It's so rare a trait these days. Unfortunately, in this particular situation, it's preventing you from grasping the magnitude of my offer." Relying only on magical influence, he hoisted me from the ground. An unseen force gripped me by the throat, causing my eyes to bulge as I kicked for freedom. "You can swear yourself to me, *or* count me as an enemy. Those are the only options available."

Casually curling one finger, he summoned me to him. My slack body floated the distance between us by no will of my own.

"This might hurt a bit," Hades warned, and stabbed his fist into my chest cavity. I could feel his digits wriggling within me, nails dragging over my spasming heart. "My strength surpasses that of Triton in ways you can't begin to comprehend. Reject me, boy, and face the full fury of Hell. Or ... avoid all that with your humble vow of servitude. I don't want to say it's a simple choice, but my pinkie finger *is* touching your spleen right now."

Chin falling to my chest, I choked out a gasp. "Mercy. Mercy, m'lord."

Retracting his hand, if only by an inch, he allowed me to suck down a breath. "Will you pledge yourself to me, Alastor?"

Knowing my options were that or death, I spat the words that left the bitter taste of loathing and regret on my tongue. "I ... pledge myself to you."

A victorious smile brightening his maliciously beatific face, Hades lowered my crumbled form to the floor.

"It really is so rewarding when a peaceful resolution can be reached." Blue wisps swirled from his fingertips. Their rolling tendrils licked at my wounds, knitting me back together and chasing away the smothering pain and exhaustion.

Clarity returned with a jolt of alarm at my newly declared fealty. Pushing up onto my elbows, I opened my eyes to a world that no longer made sense.

The ocean was gone.

What was left of Lemuria, and the sea of bodies surrounding it, had all been washed away.

In its place loomed towering trees, with their trunks twisted together in an elaborate braid. Mountains, sponged with thick tufts of green, crowned the valley around me. The crisp scent of earth and foliage replaced the stench of war.

Head snapping in one direction, then the other, I searched for answers among the flora. "Wh–what did you do? Where are we?"

"Oh, this?" Hades glanced around, as if he, too, had just noticed the change in scenery. "Hmm, it appears to be somewhere green, lovely, and far from the boundaries of Atlantica."

"You said you were going to help me." A fist of rage tightening in my gut, I pushed myself to my knees. Thankful to find my legs could hold my weight, I puffed my chest and rose in challenge before the deceitful trickster. "You said you couldn't fault me love. You healed my leg! What's the point of any of that if it doesn't return me to the water and Vanessa?"

"You foolish boy." Glaring down the bridge of his nose, Hades' lip curled back in a vicious snarl. "If it was within my capabilities to return to the sea, *don't* you think I would have done it already? Failure to do so cost me the love of my life, *and* my child. I will thank you not to assume you own the market on loss. You claim you love the girl, yet how far you'll go to find your way back to her will decide if you are worthy of her affections. Your journey begins with a day's trek in *that* direction." Folding his hands in front of him, Hades lifted his chin to the east of us. "There, you will find a kingdom welcoming to travelers."

"Why?" I spat, and took a threatening step forward. "Why would I *ever* listen to you, instead of finding my way back to the sea?"

One corner of his mouth tugging back in a sardonic smirk, Hades kept his tone calm and measured. "I'm sure you'll find basic human needs, such as food and clean water, will be quite convincing motivators. Plus, if you *did* get back to the ocean, what would you do then? Stand on the shoreline, and scream for your beloved? Serve me well, mortal, and we will both find our way back to the welcoming embrace of Mother Ocean."

The crystal around his neck pulsated once more, and Hades' form rippled. His solid stature began a slow fade into nothingness.

Lunging for him, my hand swiped through the mist that lingered were his arm had been only a moment ago. "Please, just tell me what you want from me! *What do I have to do to get home*?"

With nothing except a villainous smile left of his corporeal form, Hades chuckled. "A day's journey, hero. That's where it all begins."

CHAPTER FOUR

This was not the dabbling with humanity I underwent thanks to Vanessa's spell. During that experience I never ventured out of ear shot of Mother Ocean's steady lapping, its soothing rhythm holding the promise of home. Here, my bare feet were chaffed and bloody from the rocks and twigs I trudged over in a march to … nowhere. Every tree looked like the last. Every jog in the path thrust me farther into the maze of green. Enormous birds, larger than any I had ever seen, swooped overhead. Beaks held high, they screeched their calls at the late day sun which filtered down through slits in the canopy of leaves.

Time moved at a turtle's pace, its passing marked only by the dark shadows stretching across the damp earth. Before long, the visible slivers of sky were kissed by night's delicate violet hue. I may have found it lovely, had I not been torn from everyone and everything I cared about and experiencing crippling thirst for the very first time. Funny thing, thirst. At home it's a moot concept lost in the rolling current. Here it depleted what was left of my strength, and threatened to turn my bones to stone.

Forced to shuffle on, a vine caught my ankle and hurled me into a boulder twice the size of my head. Ribs crunched, the air leaving my lungs in a pained huff. Gasping, I rolled onto my back, and tried to blink my way through the ache. Directly above me, a splinter of moonlight illuminated a single flower. One bloom. A vision of perfection in a forest of stifling chaos. Its beauty exploded from a long stalk, silky black pedals tapering down to a blush shade of plum at the tips.

"That's a wild orchid," a playful voice taunted from everywhere, and nowhere. "Its enchanting bloom is an exotic beauty that rivals *all* other flowers. You once claimed that's what your princess was to you, did you not? It was the night before we walked ashore, and already you missed her to the depths of your core."

Pushing off my elbow, I rolled onto my knees. "Sterling? Is that you? Where are you?" My gaze swept the tree branches in search of him.

"I ... end up places." His chuckle echoed all around me; bouncing off every trunk, vibrating from the rock-covered earth. "That terrifying man with the blue-tipped hair was preparing for a jump. I thought I'd tag along. So rarely do I get to travel with company."

Craning my neck, I located him in the bend of a lofty branch. Rising to my feet, I squinted to get a better view. Only the glow of his ethereal green eyes could be seen, peering down with vexing curiosity. "I didn't understand a word of that, but perhaps we could discuss it further when you're not in a tree?"

A dry snort of disbelief wafted down from above. "I'm not in a tree. What a ludicrous— *Ow! Oof! Hunh!*"

Tumbling down from his perch, Sterling smacked several sturdy, unforgiving branches and twigs before crashing to the ground in a heap. Groaning, he flopped onto his back. "*Huh.* I was in a tree."

"Did you come back here looking for me?" I offered him a hand up, only to have him bat it away and leap up unscathed.

"That depends, who are you?" he asked, face blank of any inklings of emotion or recognition.

"Uh ... Alastor?" I offered hesitantly, wondering if this was a joke with a punchline only he was privy to. "We fought alongside each other on the beaches of Lemuria. During which time, I told you that wild orchid story you just repeated, remember?"

Jabbing his hands on his hips, Sterling's eyes narrowed. "Are those questions, or answers? Because, if *you* don't know who you are, how do you expect *me* to?"

"I *do* know! *You* acted as if *you* didn't!"

With a sympathetic shake of his head, he clucked his tongue against the roof of his mouth. Thick scars sliced his cheeks, morphing his smile into a maw of madness. "Such low self-esteem. How do you ever hope to be king?"

"I have no desire to be the king of *anything*." Pulling back, I rapidly blinked my confusion.

"Then, there's nothing to argue about." He beamed, brushing leaves from the shoulders of the frayed cloak he wore—which he definitely didn't have the last time I saw him. "You are a fickled pickle!"

My mouth opened to argue, only to be cut off by the voice of common sense pointing out what a useless cause that would be. "You're mad."

"True, but I've found all of the best people are." Digging into a newly acquired leather satchel strung across his body, he pulled out what appeared to be a red, shiny ball. After polishing it on his shirt, he tossed it to me. "After a jump, you should always find food, clothing, and water as quickly as you can. You'll learn that with time."

His claim sprouted a slew of follow-up questions, all of which were momentarily forgotten the instant the morsel settled into my palm. Mouth watering, I made myself hold back a beat. "This … is safe to eat?"

"It's called an apple. They're plentiful in most realms, and—conveniently enough—grow on trees which makes them easy to snag." Gathering an armful of small sticks, Sterling arranged them in a neat pile.

"Most realms?" I asked. Teeth bursting through the apple's outer skin, its glorious sweetness exploded in my mouth.

"You're new. You haven't seen many yet. But you will. *So many worlds, so much to see. When you return to this spot, who will you be?*" The last part he chanted to himself in a singsong voice, hands stilling from his task.

"Sterling?" I ventured, wiping my mouth on the back of my hand.

He snapped to with a jerk, picking right back up where he left off. "There's no real term for it, that I know of at least. *Jumper, Explorer, Traveler, Leaper: call it what you will, we're the real truth keepers.* I saw you down here, looking all lost and bewildered, and recognized your plight. One large piece of advice? If you insist on camping out in the open like this, you need something to deter the hungry predators prowling about. They will eagerly pounce on the chance to make a meal out of you." Shrugging off his satchel, he set it in the dirt beside him.

"Predators?" I pressed, pausing between noisy bites.

Glancing up, Sterling's lips pulled back in a wide smile that showed *all* his jagged teeth. "Meat-eating kitties and pups with sharp fangs, all with ravenous appetites."

Swallowing hard, I forced down a lump of dread with my latest mouthful.

As he snickered to himself, Sterling rubbed two sticks together until they sparked. Bowing his head, he gently blew on it until the smolder grew into a flame. "A fire will keep the beasties away while we sleep. Speaking of, your grass nappies must be getting rather scratchy by now. There's clothing in my satchel you're welcome to. If I may make a suggestion? All the worlds I have traveled in, for some reason layers translate to wisdom. I don't understand the logic, but the more I bundle the more respect and kindness I'm shown. Which is a far cry from popping up nude places. People do *not* like that one little bit. One woman threw a pigeon at me! Where did she even get the blasted thing?"

While I found it impossible to follow his zigzagged line of reasoning, a change of attire sounded incredibly appealing. When the Royal Guard prepared to burst from the sea, we girded our loins with seaweed supplied by Mother Ocean. In the time that had passed since then, it had dried to an unforgiving irritant. Translation? My bits were sore and chaffy. "Proper dress here is to cover all skin? Like you have?"

Glancing down at his ensemble, Sterling gave himself a cursory once over. His loose-fitting pants and shirt were covered by navy-blue cloak peppered with moth-eaten holes. At one hip, a wide-brimmed straw hat was tucked into his belt for later wear, on the other a canteen sagged with the weight of its cargo. "Yes," he confirmed to himself as much as me. "I covered everything. Give that a try."

Flipping open his tanned cow-hide bag, I pulled out an extra pair of pants, a shirt, and a hooded cape the same hue as the seaweed I was anxious to be rid of. "Where did you get all of this?" I asked, tugging the shirt over my head.

"I take what I need to survive, but never hurt anyone. There was a time when the guilt ate at me. Then, I got my first case of frostbite. Turns out the anguish of *that* screams louder than the nag of guilt." Freeing the canteen tied at his hip, Sterling slid it over. It bumped against the side of my foot, the contents audibly sloshing. "Drink up, you're looking a little … off."

Pondering the irony of that statement coming from *him*, I slid on the far more comfortable breeches before treating myself to a series of greedy gulps. "Where is it you're headed?" I gasped when I finally came up for air.

After throwing leaves on the growing fire, Sterling scooted back against a fallen tree trunk. "There's a kingdom not far from here that is opening its doors to all kinds—for a brief time at least. The king issued a royal decree in search of … something. I missed the details when that horrible woman began swatting me away with a broom. Still, there should at least be a hardy meal in it if the royals are hosting."

I eased myself to the ground, crossed my legs in front of me, and watched the beautiful waltz of the red and orange flames crackling toward the sky. "This kingdom, is it the only one nearby?"

"Aye." Crossing his arms, Sterling settled in with his chin to his chest.

That had to be the kingdom Hades told me about. With Sterling's help, I stood a better chance of reaching there alive. "Would you mind if I made the journey with you? New to these parts, I can't say I won't get in your way, but I'll—"

Before I could finish my sentence, Sterling's head snapped up. Lurching forward, he balanced on the balls of his feet, his wild eyes boring into mine. "You … wish to travel with me?"

"Yes?" Taken aback by the urgency of his response, I tentatively tried the answer on.

Lacing his fingers, as if in prayer, Sterling brought his knuckles to his lips. "I had people once, so very long ago. Where they are now, I fear I'll never know." Brow knit tight, he beseeched me. "If we get separated, can you stay right where you are, that I may find my way back? Can you … promise me that?" An ocean of loss and sorrow swirled in the depths of his stare, begging for an ounce of acceptance and compassion.

"Yeah." Wetting my lips, my guilty gaze shifted back to the fire. Thrust into a world I couldn't understand, how could I honor such a vow? Still, I feared denying Sterling such a request would shatter what was left of a broken man. "I promise."

"Good … good," Sterling exhaled, easing back to his resting spot. Settling in, he muttered the exact sentiment that had haunted me since the moment my feet first sank into the sand. *"Wander too far, and you can lose who you are."*

CHAPTER
FIVE

"Out of my way, appetizer!" An ogre with a drastic under-bite slammed his elbow into my shoulder in his lumber past.

Stumbling to steady my footing, I shot an exasperated glare in Sterling's direction. "What prompted the king to invite such a wayward lot to his domain?"

The second leg of our travels began before the sun crested the horizon. After a lengthy hike through the slick terrain, the peaks of the kingdom swelled before us. The closer we got, the more creatures, of every conceivable kind, swarmed the stone perimeter. While the iron gates were thrown open wide, horseback guards sifted through the crowd for those they would allow passage onto the grounds.

"It's usually either trumpeting a birth, looking for a worthy spouse, or some extravagant display to remind the rest of us that they are the exalted ones." Sterling shrugged, side-stepping to allow a grumbling troll to amble by.

Pulling up short, my hands slapped to my sides. "Wait. You don't *know*?"

Sterling's garish mouth twisted in an off-putting smirk. "Seldom is the royal decree announcing the king's search for a physically mutilated vagabond. Therefore, it doesn't really require my full attention, does it? Oh, that reminds me. Speaking of being grossly outnumbered by bone-crunching fiends—"

"We weren't, actually."

Ignoring my interjection, Sterling reached under his cloak to draw a silver-handled dagger. "I snagged this from that Huntsman who tried to choke you when you bumped his quiver."

I have dived with Great Whites, struggled from the grasp of a deadly blue octopus, and even endured the agony of fire coral. *None* of those things terrified me as much as the sight of him with a blade. "*Mother Ocean*! Why would you even *think* to do such a thing?" I gasped, ducking out of swiping range.

Turning the dagger over to inspect the gleam of its edge, his head tilted. "Figured, with us venturing into a throng of giants and brutes, one of us should be armed. And, that most certainly should *not* be me." Sterling flipped it over in his hand and offered me the weapon, handle first.

Lips parting with a pop, I gingerly closed my fingers around the grip and snatched the weapon away before he could reconsider. Tucking it into the waistband of my pants, I offered him a tight-lipped smile. "I will gladly accept a bit of protection. That gargantuan ogre keeps looking at me like I'm a snack."

"Oh, but there isn't a soul alive that can deny how delicious you are, Alastor," three sultry voices chorused in unison, injecting their alluring presence into the buzz of activity.

Conversation stopped. Bodies froze to allow one voluptuous physique to slice through the masses with her hips twitching in sassy invitation. Those ample curves were topped off by not one, not two, but *three* distinctly different heads.

One, a silky-haired exotic Asian beauty.

Two, a mocha-skinned vision with full lips and calculating eyes.

Three, a flaxen cutie with a wide smile and batting lashes.

"Hades sends his regards," One began, her voice an enticing purr.

"You've done well following his instruction." Two batted impossibly long lashes, her lips pursed in a knowing grin.

"Now, allow us to bestow a gift of his gratitude," Three finished, her neck stretching and rolling.

"Don't look them in the eye!" Sterling shrieked. Spinning away from the curvy strumpets, he shielded his face behind his arms.

"You know what they are?" Following his instruction, I clapped a hand over my eyes.

"Not in the least. But if there is even a slight chance they could devour my soul and lay eggs in my skull, I'm all for the closed eye strategy." Blindly swinging at the air, Sterling swatted them away. "Away, beast! Return to your sensual, nubile hell!"

Cursing myself for listening to him, I dropped my hand. To my surprise, the three-headed temptress shrank back into the crowd with laughter bubbling from their lips.

Peeking through his fingers, Sterling's arms drooped an iota. "*Huh.* I did *not* think that would work."

"It didn't." Tensing, my hand twitched over the hilt of the dagger.

Necks lengthening, the three heads moved with serpent fluidity, slithering and swaying in search of their prey. Utilizing the same approach, Three chose a boil-marked troll. Locking stares with him, she murmured inaudible sentiments that made his breath catch. Tongue darting out to wet her lower lip, One targeted a centaur. Meanwhile, Two spoke soft and sweet to the ill-tempered ogre.

I wasn't privy to the promises or incantations they uttered. I didn't have to be. The punch of their impact resonated with a force that knocked the air from my lungs.

"Kill them for me," all three simultaneously crooned.

Bedlam erupted in response. With a high-pitched caterwaul, a troll tackled an unsuspecting dwarf. Rolling across the ground, the two punched, and kicked at any soft tissue where they could land a blow. Behind them, a centaur mule kicked two bushy-bearded ruffians. The two flew back, bowling over on-lookers before slumping to the ground in a heap of tangled limbs. Stepping over their crumpled forms, a grey-pallored ogre stomped straight for a shriveled hag who protected herself by throwing a potion in his face. A spray of magical magenta sparks cursed him with a pig snout, and a curly pink tail. Beaming in triumph, the three-headed she-devil sunk into the forest's overgrowth, allowing the foliage to swallow them whole.

Violence and magic winging all around, a coven of women and children—recognizable by the pewter pentacle pendants strung around their necks—huddled together in the midst of the waylay. Hiding behind the skirts of their mothers, the terror on the faces of the young whispered to my warrior instincts. Shoving my way through the scuffle, I blazed a path to their aid.

"Are you all able to move?" I pressed, rounding my back to shield them from an airborne hob-goblin.

Hands clasped in a protective circle, subtle nods from the sisterhood were the only response they offered.

"Good. Stay close to me. I'll get you out of here." I started to turn, only to be halted by a tender hand on my forearm.

"Child," the elder of the coven, with greying hair at her temples, beseeched me, "come into the circle."

Setting my jaw to the task, I squared my shoulders for battle. "No, m'lady. I'm here to secure you safe passage."

As if sent to challenge that claim, a gnarled twig of a man stumbled up beside me. Reaching for a waifish redhead in the folds of the coven, he slurred through missing and rotted teeth, "Such untouched innocence. Give us a kiss, lass."

Drunk on purpose, I flipped the dagger over with a swirl of my fingers. Palming it in an overhand grip, I swung wide, stopping close enough to shave his neck in the most final of ways. "Step away from her."

The man's eyes, rimmed yellow from obvious abuse of spirits, shifted to my blade. His unruly brows knit tight. "There are many men here with growing needs and insatiable appetites. Do you think you can protect them all?"

"Show me one among you that couldn't be cut down with a well-aimed swipe," I growled, lips curling from my teeth.

Corners of his eyes crinkling, the overly-sauced man stuck two fingers in his mouth and pierced the hush with an ear-piercing whistle.

"*Appetizer!*" the ogre who bumped me earlier bellowed. The earth trembled as the colossal beast charged straight for me.

"While he's batting you around, I'll make friends with your charges." Yellow-eyes snickered, making disgusting kissy noises to the ladies behind me. Luckily, they were too focused on their chanting to pay him any mind.

"Sterling!" I shouted, middle finger drumming my agitation against the hilt of the dagger at my hip. "A bit of help would be appreciated!"

He lingered on the edge of the chaos, watching with a spectator's enthusiasm. Every punch thrown, elbow to the gut, or knee to the nose earned an awestruck gasp of appreciation.

"*Sterling!*" I hollered a second time.

"Alastor, my friend and traveling partner!" he shouted back, not blinking out of fear he might miss something. "Are you seeing this?"

Tongue lolling from his mouth, the ogre licked his lips with a noisy smack. His hands hungrily reached for me as he clomped closer still.

"Sure am!" I yelped, fighting the urge to squeeze my eyes shut before being eaten alive by the giant monstrosity. "Little help here?"

"*Oh!*" Throwing open his satchel, Sterling's head disappeared inside the bag. "I have just the thing!" Rustling around within the confines of the fabric, he emerged with … a wood flute.

Yellow-eyes howled with laughter, clutching his side in between peals.

Not ready to accept the bone-crunching to come, I assumed a defensive stance and pulled my blade. "What's the plan, Sterling? You going to throw that thing at him?"

"How would that be helpful?" Sterling mocked with a snort, and brought the flute to his lips. While I feared a grisly, bloody death, he coaxed an up-beat melody from the instrument.

Under the weighty yoke of his lunacy, my shoulders sank. "Music to be eaten by. That's helpful. Thank you."

Eyebrows raised, Sterling nodded exuberantly in between soothing toots.

"The eye, go for the ogre's eye." The grey-haired Wiccan nudged me forward with an elbow to the kidney.

"Sterling!" I barked in one last ditch effort, cringing as the ogre arched back for attack.

His response?

To play faster, with a bit more pep.

Clenching my teeth in preparation for the first strike, a flash of yellow streaked by close enough to blow my hair back. Drawn to the music, the darting orb zipped around Sterling, bobbing and dipping in time with the tune. The light lilt of laughter rode the breeze behind it, dousing the belligerent crowd with a calming air of innocence. Fists froze mid-punch. Bites morphed into perplexed frowns. Stabs, intended to be deadly, opted merely for flesh wounds. As a blanketed hush fell across the courtyard, all eyes locked on the nymph materializing beside Sterling in a spray of twinkling white light. Wearing a gown of leaves that whispered over her curves, a halo of wildflowers decorated the snow-white hair falling in messy waves to her waist. Eyes, the bright green of freshly sprouted moss, crinkled at the corners as she lifted her shoulders with a dainty giggle.

One as delicate as she *should* have shrunk from the heaving ogre. Nevertheless, she glided to his side, moving with the simplistic grace of a feather on a breeze. Placing her hand on the thick boulder of his forearm, she blinked up at him with a face full of trust and acceptance.

"If you act in darkness, you're no better than those that hurt you," she said, her voice the sweet melody of a tinkling bell.

The ogre chewed on her statement before snorting through flared nostrils and stomping off into the tree line. Ground shaking under his substantial stride, he didn't slow or glance back.

Work not yet complete, the nymph pranced to the side of the yellow-eyed drunk. "Samuel, this won't bring her back."

I expected him to sneer. To scoff at such a foolish attempt at distraction. To my shock, his face crumbled. Shoulders shaking with vigorous sobs, he folded into her welcoming embrace. In between hiccups, he muttered thanks to the wild beauty that cleansed his tarnished heart.

Gifting her his treasured flask, yellow-eyes sulked off with whimpers still leaking from his quivering lips. It was then that the nymph turned my way, gracing me with the beaming warmth of her smile.

She skipped the distance between us, then pressed two fingers to my wrist, urging me to lower my weapon. "Alastor," head listing to the side, flaxen hair swept from her shoulders in an exquisite veil, "he had *no one* before you."

"B–but … I barely know the bloke," I stammered, rapidly blinking my confusion.

As the sun sunk in the sky, torches were lit along the castle walls that illuminated the nymph's hair with a halo of sparkling gold. "It's time … to start believing in yourself."

Further questions were forming on my lips when a sharp trumpet blast cut through the night, demanding the attention of the crowd.

A spray of sparkles and the nymph disappeared.

"You there, hero!" an armor-clad soldier called from horseback. "Was your valiant display worthy of the commotion it caused?"

Lifting my chin with an air of defiance, I owned my actions. "Aye. I will never stand idly by while the weak and downtrodden are victimized."

"Weak?" The guard chuckled, straightening in his saddle. "Perhaps you should ask the sisterhood how they feel about being described in such fashion."

"I'm sure they appreciate me acting in ..." Glancing over my shoulder, I trailed off. The entire coven was gone. If I had to guess, I would wager it was thanks to a spell they didn't need me, or my bolstered bravado, to evoke.

"You must be new to these parts. People of the Kingdom of Caselotti quickly learn that the sisters are among the most powerful of our residents." Steadying his side-stepping stallion, his eyes narrowed in judgement. "How was it you summoned the nymph? Do you possess magics of your own?"

"No, sir. Fortunately, my traveling companion knew how to summon her with a song."

In the process of stowing away his flute, Sterling hummed a merry little tune, oblivious to being mentioned.

After exchanging conspiratorial glances with the guard opposite him, the soldier offered me a forced smile. "The king is done meeting with his subjects for tonight. However, for your attempted chivalry, we can allow you and your friend to sleep in the royal stable if you are without shelter this night."

"It's that, or the forest floor. We graciously accept the invitation." Catching Sterling by the elbow, I guided him alongside me as we followed the soldiers inside the imposing walls of the kingdom.

Glancing from my grip on his arm, to my face, Sterling brightened. "Alastor! It's so good to see you! I just played a *grand* concert! The wine flowed, and people danced and twirled into the wee hours of the night. One fresh-faced maiden even lost her slipper."

"What a wonderful performance that must have been," I muttered, through my teeth.

Every word from the little imp's mouth was more befuddling then the last, yet the nymph claimed he was lost without me. I would guide him. Travel with him. Help him in any way I could. Even so, if faced with the chance to return to the sea, I couldn't allow guilt over a mad stranger prevent me from following my heart.

Lying on a bed of straw, I stared up at the night sky and contemplated how I became the pawn of a demi-god. Hades maneuvered me where he saw fit, and I allowed it. Why? Because love is an intoxicating distraction impossible to ignore.

Huddled across the stall from me, Sterling challenged a pregnant sow in a battle to determine which could snore the loudest.

Had it not been for their rhythmic onslaught, I may have slept through the parade of soft, floating lights gliding past the barn. Drawn to their glow, I pushed myself from the ground in a crunch of snapped stalks, and crouched alongside a sleeping goat to peer out. Six cloaked figures drifted in circles, swaying and dipping. Their cadenced waltz honored the flickering flames of lanterns cradled in their palms. Faster and faster they moved, the poetry of their dance eliciting an energy that crackled through the square.

Momentum reaching a fevered pitch, one among them stabbed her lantern toward the sky. Taking the cue, the others responded in turn. Like shooting stars, each lantern lifted from the fingertips of their host to become part of night's bejeweled cloak.

"That's it then?" a timid male voice interjected, breaking the spell of their prancing pirouettes.

The figure who led the ritual stepped forward, shrugging off her hood.

Craning to see over the slotted barn wood, I recognized her as the grey-haired woman from the coven. Not knowing much about their craft, I guessed her to be their High Priestess.

"When the sun sets tomorrow evening, the chosen oracle will awaken to his call," she stated in a clipped tone, folding her hands in front of her.

The mysterious man raised one hand, as if to reach for her. Thinking better of it, he closed it into a tight fist and let it drop to his side. "And ... we're sure this lad will do? He is noble of heart?"

Titters of amusement from her coven earned a silencing scowl from the Priestess. "Had you seen his actions in the courtyard, you wouldn't think to doubt me."

An icy chill skittered down my spine. For reasons I couldn't explain, I knew without a shadow of doubt they were talking about me. It seemed Hades wasn't the only one herding me in the direction he desired.

"I would never —" the man countered, only to be cut off by the Priestess' raised hand.

"This *awakening*," she interrupted, "comes with a warning. The oracle and the trickster are bound by nature's balance. When you strengthen one, the other is equally bolstered."

"The trickster?" the man reiterated, taking a step back into the shadows.

"Varying cultures refer to them by a plethora of titles." A nod from their priestess and the coven began gathering their lanterns and supplies. "Tricksters, Menehune, leprechauns; to name a few. All refer to the same mischievous spirits. While the oracle will guide, the trickster's talent lies in unfathomable atrocities. None in your kingdom will be safe until *both* entities are banished from these lands."

"I can't banish the oracle until the artifact is recovered!" the man erupted, pacing a trench into the castle square. "Elsewise this will all be for naught. There must be a way to contain the Trickster. How do I identify this malicious spirit?"

A smile snaked across her lips, coiling at the corners. "Make no mistake, Your Majesty, *they* will find *you*."

Light—as bright as midday sun—flashed, and the coven was gone.

In their absence, a powerful urge to sleep blanketed me. It claimed me before my lashes could brush my cheeks, leaving my body to crumble atop the snoozing goat.

CHAPTER SIX

Throw him in the stocks!" a commanding voice boomed.

"No, please! I meant no harm! Sometimes, I just ... *end up places!"* Sterling shrieked, his feet dragging over the ground.

"*End up places?*" Holding him by the arms, the soldiers forced him forward. "You were in the nursery of the infant princess. That is dastardly, deliberate, and you shall pay dearly for it."

Slapped awake by their shouts, I pushed from the straw-covered ground and stumbled to the stall door through a thick cloud of grogginess.

"I was in the nursery of the princess?" Sterling scowled, visibly perplexed by such an accusation. A crowd had begun to form in the square, the sounds of their scuffle waking the sleeping court. A beat later Sterling's eyes brightened. "Ah, yes! I was in the nursery of the princess!"

"He admits it!"

"To the stocks with him!"

"The king will have his head!" The armor-clad soldiers shouted over each other.

I took a step toward helping him, only to be hit by a powerful wave of vertigo. Hand gripping the door frame, I struggled to steady myself. My eyes. Something was wrong with my eyes. Blinking hard, I squinted to focus.

"*Alastor*! There's my friend Alastor!" Limp feet thumping up the stairs, Sterling was heaved onto the raised platform of the stocks. "Tell them! Tell them about my affliction!"

Pushing off the door, I staggered out through the haze causing my temples to pound. "He ... slends up paces," was the best my thick tongue could slur.

"Compelling counterpoint, by the drunk," one of the soldiers sneered, shoving Sterling forward with more force than necessary.

Blinking hard, I opened my eyes to a world of starbursts and strobing colors. Jaw swinging slack, I marveled at the flashes of pink and purple pulsating around Sterling in a hypnotic current. The soldiers manhandling him were haloed by a pulse of red flaring around them. Every person my stare swung to reflected another variation of a color.

While I was momentarily frozen by this newfound rainbow, Sterling's head was snapped forward by an elbow to the skull. "Gents, please! If you could just give me a moment, this can all be explained as the innocent act it was!"

"You can tell us all about it, while you're locked up and baking in the midday sun!" the husky guard with a red, wiry beard growled. Gritting his teeth, he attempted to shove Sterling into the binding contraption, only to have him wriggle from his grasp.

"I would really prefer we talk beforehand." Squeezing his eyes shut, Sterling vanished with an audible *pop*. While the guards holding him fumbled to regain their footing, he reappeared perched crosslegged atop of the stocks. "Am I back? Is all of me here?"

"Commander, he has magic!" A young soldier with a rash of freckles yelped, reaching for his sword.

"I do?" Sterling pulled back, arms pinwheeling to keep his balance. "How wonderful! What kind?"

"Get down at once!" red-beard rumbled. Hand curling around one of the support posts, he scanned the contraption for his own way up.

"Gladly, just as soon as you stop trying to stick my head in things," Sterling bargained with an enthusiastic nod.

Using one of the arm restraints as a foothold, Red-beard heaved himself up with a series of strained grunts. "No such agreement will be made. You will come down and face your sentencing like a man!"

The instant his hand closed around Sterling's ankle, the enigmatic imp disappeared yet again. This time he solidified on top of the castle wall. Patting himself down, he did a cursory scan to ensure all his parts made the journey with him. "Bugger, my pants are on backwards. Hope the bits underneath are still facing the proper way."

"Enough of these foolish games!" Jumping down from the stocks, the captain's boots slammed against the wooden platform, kicking up a cloud of dust. "Archers, take aim! Come down, son, or we will shoot you down!"

As the soldiers readied their weapons, the crimson light enveloping them throbbed with waves of inky black. My stomach knotted with the palpable malice of their intent, acidic rancor scorching up my throat.

"Such a ruckus so early in the day," a voice, which rang with familiarity, chortled from the castle's grand door. "What seems to be the trouble?"

Without hesitation, every soldier took a knee. Every head bowed. Except for mine, because I was busy watching the light track from my own hand. And Sterling's, because he was introducing himself to a butterfly. Not a proud moment for either of us.

"Your Majesty," Red-beard spoke to the ground, "that loon atop the wall was found in the princess' nursery this morning. We meant only to hold him until you could question him on his intentions, and rule accordingly."

"My intentions?" Sterling asked the butterfly, as if the insect was questioning his character. "She's but a *bairn*. My lone intent was to protect her."

Folding his hands before his slight frame, the man I now realized to be the king tilted his head. Thick hair, streaked with grey, spilled over his shoulders. The shimmer buzzing around him, for my eyes only, glowed a vibrant amethyst. "Protect her from what?"

As he posed the question, a petite beauty edged up behind him. Her lips were the brilliant red of a freshly bloomed rose. Hair polished ebony. Skin the soft pallet of fresh fallen snow. However, none of those elements could touch the enchanting white light resonating out of this captivating creature. In her arms, she cradled a cherub-faced baby cooing and squirming in a yellow nightgown with red and blue piping.

"Liam, you need to stop this," the woman I guessed to be his queen demanded, shifting the baby from one hip to the other.

Sterling danced a precarious circle on the ledge, bouncing on the balls of his feet. "The queen! Ever so late! Yet, she's here. Her watch must be set two days behind." Jerking at his own rambling, the point of his chin twitched to the side. "But, there are no watches here, are there? It would be so nice if something made sense for a change."

King Liam tensed at the disconcerting news it fell to him to deliver. "I can't, dear heart. It seems the guards found this man in Princess Snow's nursery this morning."

Finally finding my voice, I dragged my leaden feet forward. "I can vouch for him. He's a bit … eccentric, but he wouldn't harm anyone." The words soured on my tongue, sorely lacking the flavor of truth. I barely knew the man. What he was doing in that child's room, I dreaded to think. But if I didn't speak in his favor, who would?

"*I know*, I was there," the queen nonchalantly admitted, as if plucking the doubt from my mind and crushing it between her bejeweled fingers.

The clustered audience sucked in a shocked gasp at the drama unfolding.

Their king, on the other hand, was far from amused. Chest swelling, he spun on his queen, frantic gaze inspecting every inch of her. "Evelyn! Why is this the first I'm hearing of this? Are you okay?"

"We are both *fine*," she clarified, clucking at the grinning infant. "I fell asleep on the lounge in her room, and woke to a lovely song our new friend was crooning to little Snow. He didn't touch her. Didn't reach for her. Just peered down, and sang a sweet tune. Truth be told, I thought it was a dream, until the guards burst in. A fact we both need to consider, Liam, is that he had time and opportunity to hurt us if that was his intent. Fortunately, he did not. I'm of the mind to accept that blessing and hear him out. Or, at the very least, find out how he got so deep into the castle without alerting our slew of soldiers."

The guards and spectators fell silent, waiting with breathless anticipation for the king's reaction.

Brow knit in a deep V of concern, King Liam warned, "If anything had happened to either of you …"

Placing her palm over his heart, Queen Evelyn murmured in a soothing caress, "Love, it *didn't.*"

"Neither lass was ever in any danger!" Sterling crowed. One step forward and he tumbled off the wall's edge. Screeching as he fell, he landed in a low crouch that surprised even him. He bounced to his feet, pouncing on his point before it evaded him. "That's why I was there. To protect the baby. Cures … cures are hard to find. A pill here. A vial there. Eat me. Drink me. There's no way to know. No way to be certain. Prevention is key, and good advice indeed."

"Florencio," lip curling in distain, King Liam called to Redbeard, "have you any idea what this interloper is trying to say?"

"Not in the least, Majesty." A roll of his shoulders caused Florencio's armor to shift and clap. "I think he's quite mad."

Exchanging brooding glares, the energy surrounding the king and his men hissed and crackled. Their alarm festered into fingers of red and orange that clawed around them in vicious warning.

Shifting her hold on the baby, Queen Evelyn ignored her husband's glower and delivered the princess into his arms. "Keep the swords sheathed, lads. Let's pretend to be civilized and try diplomacy over bloodshed." Heels clicking over the cobblestone portico, she lifted the hem of her gown and descended the stairs. "What is your name, friend?"

Eyes wide and manic, Sterling blinked his astonishment that someone actually wanted to listen to him. "Sterling, ma'am."

Closing the distance between them, she greeted him with a warm smile. "It's a pleasure to put a name to that lovely serenade, Sterling. Could you tell me what it was you felt you needed to protect the princess from?"

Wetting his lips, his head twitched side to side, rifling through the chaos in his mind for the needed information. "Sickness comes for sweet Snow. Brought by one you're yet to know. Take from no strangers any offered loot. Threat comes in the form of … No, that can't be right." Sterling chewed on the inside of his cheek, second-guessing the path this line of thought had led him down. Looking to the queen, his stare pleaded for understanding. "Fruit? Threat comes in the form of fruit?"

Glassy silence followed, only to be shattered by sharp peals of laughter. The square came alive with guffaws at Sterling's expense. Each thrown-back head and pointed finger shrank him further in on himself.

Queen Evelyn maintained a maternal compassion. Stepping closer, she gave his arm a comforting squeeze. "Where did you get this information from? Maybe if we look there we can solve this mystery together?"

Face crumbling, Sterling blinked back a wash of tears. "I've spilled the tea and now I'm not invited to the party." Grey waves of crestfallen frustration oozed from him, spawned by his inability to find the right words.

Answering his silent scream for help, I cleared my throat to speak over the titters of laughter. "As the queen attested to, this man is no threat. If you release him into my care, we will take our leave."

The laughter died on King Liam's lips, his eyes narrowing with recognition. "If it isn't the hero from yesterday's ruckus in the courtyard." Energy melding to a deep plum, the king passed the princess to Florencio and trotted down the stairs. "Tell me, lad, this traveling companion of yours, do you see good in him?"

Feeling the heat of Sterling's stare boring into the side of my face, I lifted my chin to the king. "He may seem a bit eccentric, but he's hurt no one."

Inching closer, the king's shoulders lifted to his ears in a dismissive shrug. "I don't believe that's what I asked. Look at him. Can you *see* his goodness?"

I dragged my tongue over my teeth, white-washing my face of growing unease. "I saw as you did, my Lord. That his misguided efforts were meant to help. After all, isn't that the closest to insight any of us can achieve?"

Folding his hands as if in prayer, the king pressed his knuckles to his bearded chin. "In ancient scribes there are mentions of oracles who can see the truth within another. Perhaps you possess such a nature?"

"Liam, what do such inane ponderings matter? No harm has been done. Let's let them go, and return to our breakfast. Linger much longer, and your favorite cheese biscuits will be cold."

Princess Snow began to fuss, prompting Queen Evelyn to wave Florencio over with her. Honoring her command, he handed over the royal treasure awkwardly nestled in his chainmail clad arms.

"In good time, dearest!" Liam waggled one finger over his head. "I indulged your inquiry. Humor mine for a moment, won't you? I long to learn more about the noble man who makes a habit of swooping in to save others. Tell me, hero, do you know this Sterling? Is he friend, or family to you?"

"This reality is frightening." Edging up beside me, Sterling pinched the fabric of my sleeve between his fingers and gave it a tug. "My only weapon is my imagination, and I fear that blade is dull."

"Neither, Your Highness. We met briefly before," I confirmed. "Even fought alongside each other as brothers in war. I hate to disappoint you, but I'm just a simple-minded fool who chooses to see the good in people."

"Someone armed that aberration?" Florencio snorted.

Maintaining an eerie calm, King Liam's tone dropped to a measured purr. "I wonder if what you refer to as simple, is untested talents? Perhaps a trial of sorts is in order?"

Queen Evelyn rested the baby on her cocked hip, her almond-shaped eyes narrowing. "Liam—love of my life, wise and noble king of Caselotti—what the blazes are you doing?"

"All in good fun, my Queen. I'm sure our new friend wouldn't mind a demonstration. Let's start with," the king's breath caught, a devilish glint crinkling the corners of his eyes, "my wife. Use this clairvoyance of yours. Read our beloved queen, and tell me what you see."

Squaring her shoulders, Evelyn's jaw tensed. "Liam, whatever you're playing at, stop at once."

Before my gaze swung her way, I made up my mind not to acknowledge the newfound lights I could sense. Not when Sterling's display of magical talents had been met with hostile alarm. Then, I looked at the striking queen. Really looked at her. That haloing glow, mesmerizing with its twinkling purity, faded around the edges. Rippling out, her wholesome white faded into murky wafts. Each wave hinted at an essence soon to be snuffed out.

Stunned by the revelation, the words tumbled from my lips before I could think to filter them. "She's sick."

While those two words earned a gasp from the onlookers, a victorious smirk tugged at the corner of the king's mouth.

The world slowed to a crawl, a dull roar screaming in my ears. "You knew," I rasped to the scheming king. "You were the one hidden in the shadows of the square last night, watching the priestess conjure her spell."

Evelyn's flawless forehead puckered. "Liam, what is he talking about?"

Thumbing my nose at royal etiquette, I stepped chest to chest with the king. Triggered by my advance, his men drew their swords. "You'll be on your back before they take one step," I growled. "What the hell did you do to me, and *why?*"

"Sheath your swords," Liam ordered his men, his cadence oddly serene and accepting. When Florencio hesitated, the king tore his stare from mine to address his man. "Clear the square, at once."

"Yes, Your Highness." A nod to his fellow soldiers, and Florencio hopped to his task of waving spectators back to their homes.

"I will be up to feed her shortly," Queen Evelyn murmured to the handmaid who scurried over to collect the princess.

Lips pressed in a thin line, Liam waited for the footfalls to pad off in various directions before answering to my demands. "My wife ... is dying," he admitted, voice cracking with emotion. "We have revealed to the kingdom that she's ill, but have kept the true nature of her condition quiet."

"At my request," Evelyn added, taking her husband's arm.

Linking the fingers of his free hand with hers, Liam dotted a tender kiss between her knuckles. "There's legend of a mirror," he continued. "A timeless artifact that possesses all truth. Any question will be answered, as long as posed by one noble of heart, and blessed with the gift of sight. I opened the doors to the kingdom, and planted a few disorderly characters in hopes a champion would be uncovered. And you were. Through magical influence it was possible to add the second needed attribute." Pivoting on the ball of his foot, the king beseeched his queen. "Evelyn, don't you see? This could be the key to restoring your health!"

"*You cursed an unsuspecting stranger?*" Eyes bulging, Evelyn blinked in disbelief.

"I would do this and worse to keep you safe," Liam explained, desperation snaking through his bold statement. "His quest will be a simple one! He merely needs to recover the artifact, and bring it back that we may retrieve our answers!"

"And if I were to say no?" I asked, drumming my fingers over the hilt of my dagger.

As the queen jabbed her hands on her hips, her brow hitched in anticipation of his response.

Tongue dragging over his lower lip, King Liam uttered the potential consequences as if they pained him. "Of course, you will be free to go if you so choose. Your friend, however, *did* trespass in the castle. I'm afraid he will have to stay and answer for his crimes."

She shook her head, the exertion from the conflict draining her complexion waxen. "Liam, I am horrified, and beyond disappointed in you."

Catching her hands in his, Liam ducked his head to draw her reluctant regard back to his face. "I acted in desperation! I won't deny that. But I did so because I can't fathom living in a world without you in it. No lives have been harmed or risked. Yet, a treasured one could be saved if it works. I can't, and won't, be sorry for that."

Pulling her hands away, Evelyn's chin trembled. "You are so wrong about that, my love. One *is* at risk. Yours. As the kind and gentle man who stole my heart."

Their touching moment registered as little more than background noise to the deafening buzz reverberating in my mind. With detached numbness, I let my stare sweep over the kingdom. The castle loomed before me, a towering jewel of regal pageantry. On the remaining three sides, shops and humble homes nestled against the rock wall.

"So far from home," I mused to myself more than the squabbling royals. "Yet, so much is still the same. Both are ruled by those charged with making lofty decisions that dictate the lives of others. I wouldn't be here now if a young king didn't feel pressured to protect his precious throne."

"How horrible," Evelyn fretted, her hand fluttering to the jewels strung round her neck.

"I'm not in search of pity. I simply need you to understand that I recognize the desire to protect the people you hold dear, at all cost. I will honor the king's request to find this mirror for two reasons. First, if it was my love, Vanessa, I wouldn't stop until I found a way to save her, same as you. Secondly," throwing my arms out wide, I huffed a humorless laugh, "I understand my position here, and that I have no real choice in this matter."

"While the situation isn't nearly as bleak as you make it sound, I cannot begin to describe how grateful we would be to have you as our oracle." Liam perked at his victory, aglow with hopeful promise. I fully intended to scrub the joy from his face.

Holding up one finger, I waved it thrice before pressing it to my lips. "That reminds me. There was *one* more question I had about the magic you called upon to commandeer my life. After the lovely choreography, the High Priestess made mention of a trickster being summoned along with me, that was capable of … how did she put it? *Unfathomable atrocities.* What was that all about?"

King Liam paled, mouth opening and closing in search of a workable explanation. "Evelyn, I can explain. It was a necessary evil for the greater good."

"I need you to stop talking." his queen snapped. Bowing her head, she dragged the back of her hand over her sweat dampened brow. Lips paling to a dusky beige, bruise like shadows sprouted under her eyes. "We will go inside, and find these gentlemen adequate accommodations for the duration of their stay. After which, I will take a brief rest and then seek you out, *my husband*, for a *long* overdue conversation."

CHAPTER SEVEN

T ell us more about Atlantica," one of the three breathy hand-
maidens, tasked with making me pass for a gentleman,
requested.

Their hands flittered all around me. Combing and pinning
back my hair. Shaving my face. Fastening some sort of floppy tie
around my neck. They claimed it accentuated my shirt and hand-
stitched jacket. I thought it closer resembled a jellyfish attacking my
throat.

Gazing into the vanity table mirror, I leaned back in my chair
and studied the pseudo-human peering back. "Humans are
beautiful. Truly, you are."

All three of them tittered with girlish giggles, the light of their
auras blooming bright carnation pink.

"Even so, underwater," I continued, getting lost in my own
reverie, "the skin of every mer glistens in the floating diamonds of
the filtered light. Hair dances and flows around every face, as if
there for the sole purpose of framing the loveliness of the being it
adorns."

Hairbrushes stilled.

Fabric fluffing fingers paused.

The gleam of the straight blade hovered mid-swipe.

A chorus of dreamy sighs escaped the parted lips of each lady tending to me.

"Touched by Mother Ocean's artistic pallet, hair isn't merely black. It is an inky luminescence that pays loving tribute to every color under the rainbow. Eyes aren't simply purple. They are treasured amethysts rediscovered by the mysteries of the depths." So lost was I in the mirage of my mind, that the image of Vanessa was conjured behind my lids. Each blink, momentarily taunted me with my soul's desire.

"You have the heart of a poet, sir," the tallest of the three girls gasped, resuming her task of crisscrossing my hair into a braided rope.

"Not to mention being dreamy," the platinum-haired lass with the blade at my throat breathed.

"Claudette!" the third of the trio, adjusting my tie, snapped. Her foot stomped for emphasis.

"What?" The girl I now knew as Claudette let her shoulder rise and fall in a shrug. "There is a mirror right in front of him, Laurette. He *knows* what he looks like."

"You don't speak of such things!" Laurette huffed, cheeks reddening.

"No, *you* don't speak of such things. *I* acknowledge the blatantly obvious." Claudette winked at me in the mirror.

"And I am sure our guest appreciates such flattery," a crisp voice proclaimed from the doorway.

In an instant, the trio moved shoulder to shoulder, dipping in curtsies of respect.

"Your Highness," they chorused in acknowledgment of their queen.

"You may rise." Lifting her chin in their direction, she adjusted the cooing princess balanced on her hip. That simple task seemed taxing on her waning strength, causing the infant to sink from her hold.

Bounding from my seat, I caught the tyke under her chubby little arms. I drew her to me and cradled her against my chest. "Good evening, Princess. How fare you this night?"

Puffing her rosy cheeks, she blew spit bubbles in response.

"I couldn't have said it better myself!" I chuckled, pulling my face back to avoid a flailing baby fist.

Black ringlets haloing her porcelain face, Snow blinked up at me beneath her forest of lashes. Gracing me with a toothless grin, she mashed her fist into her mouth and gnawed on it.

Queen Evelyn offered a tight-lipped smile to her maidens as she eased herself into the seat I vacated. "We are fine, ladies. You're excused."

Bowing once more, they scurried from the room, careful not to insult their queen by turning their backs to her.

The elegant royal waited for the door to shut behind them before fixing her steely-eyed scrutiny my way. "Out of respect for both of our time, I'm going to cut right to it. I apologize for the situation my husband has put you in. While an incredibly sweet man, he can be maddeningly stubborn."

"When it comes to you, it's easy to see he acts out of love, Your Highness," I responded. Doing my impression of a puffer fish, I earned a giggle of delight from the princess.

"Call me Evelyn, please."

"As you wish, Queen Evelyn."

Crossing her legs at the ankle, her gaze drifted to her daughter and happily lingered there. "He loves me, and is so terrified of what's to come that it prevents him from accepting the truth of how far my illness has progressed. You reached for the princess because you feared I would drop her. Even you, a stranger, can see I'm wilting."

"I did," I admitted with a nod of regret.

"And I thank you for that. Heaven knows those three clucking hens wouldn't have noticed unless she hit the floor and bounced." Seeing Snow beginning to pout, Evelyn reached for her. I stepped forward, delivering the precious cargo onto her mother's lap. "My husband has implored every healer in the realm in search of a cure. No one has been able to identify the ailment, much less offer up a remedy. Still, Liam refuses to give up."

"Because he loves you," I muttered, begrudgingly finding myself sympathetic to his plight. "Once you've given your soul to someone, there's no limit to how far you will go on their behalf."

"Yes," the queen stated, eyes narrowing as if seeing me for the first time, "I do believe you understand that caliber of affection. When he heard rumors of the mirror, it became a bit of an obsession for him. It always seemed a fool's errand to me, a proverbial magic bean, he would grow tired of when he saw it for the pointless endeavor it was. Had I known he was still pursuing the notion, I would have stopped him before things escalated to this point. While his heart is in the right place, I wish he could find peace in the inevitable truth."

"And what's that?" I asked, leaning one hip against the vanity table.

Lifting her chin, the dancing light from the oil lamp cast deep shadows over Evelyn's sunken cheeks. "That there are some elements of life we cannot change or fight."

With a lump of unease coiling in my gut, I ran the palm of my hand over my freshly shaved chin. "I'm not sure I'm comfortable with where this conversation is headed."

Raising her eyebrows, the queen thrilled her daughter by adopting a high-pitched chirp. "Nor should you be. This is a very perplexing matter. *Yes, it is! Yes, it is!*" Beaming at Snow's belly laugh, Evelyn eased her into the crook of her arm, and turned to face me. "I need you to promise me, no matter where this journey takes you, that you will *not* take any unnecessary risks. Your safety is more important than a desperate man's quest for a miracle."

Crossing to her in two wide strides, I took a knee before the fading queen. "M'lady, you are as compassionate as you are lovely. I can see why he fights so ruthlessly for you. It is my honor to be chosen not only as your oracle, but your champion on this quest for answers."

The smile vanished from Evelyn's face, replaced by a stern, unforgiving stare. "Then you aren't listening. The *only* help I desire from you is a vow to look out for my daughter, husband, and kingdom after I'm gone."

I opened my mouth to argue, only to be hushed by her finger to my lips. "Go on this journey. Use it to search for your path home. But, please, don't allow yourself to be saddled with the burden of my affliction."

Before I could formulate an argument, Queen Evelyn hoisted Snow onto her hip and swept from the room without another word.

CHAPTER EIGHT

Glasses clinked. Cutlery scraped over plates. Decadent food was wheeled out by the cartful. The dining table stretched the length of the expansive hall, decorated with gold and silver finery. A candle chandelier, dripping with diamonds, hung overhead, warming those below with its golden shimmer.

Clothing and costuming options were limited under the sea. I mean, there's only so much you can do with seaweed, squid ink, and pearls. Here, the regalia of each person was surpassed by the next. Before entering the dinner thrown in my honor, I thought my silken coat—the shade of soft sand and trimmed with navy embroidery—to be a fetching one. In that ostentatious crowd it seemed dull by comparison.

At the head of the table, King Liam swigged from his goblet of wine and mulled over his plans with the trusted members of his court ... along with Sterling and me. "Our research has shown the mirror's last known whereabouts to be a pirate refuge known as Marooner's Rock. While we have a map, scouts and travelers claim it to be a fake, as they have never encountered any of the landmarks at the labeled coordinates during their travels."

"Mmmmmm," Sterling interrupted. Soaking up the decadent gravy on his plate with what was left of his bread, he popped it in his mouth and slurped the remnants from each fingertip before he innocently inquired, "I'm terribly sorry, I forgot to ask this earlier, but … are you a moron?"

Queen Evelyn nearly choked on her potatoes, covering her mouth before she sprayed them across the table.

Clamping his lips together, Liam blinked in Sterling's direction as if considering whether to listen, or have him killed. "You had something to add, young man?"

"You seek something but know not where. Reflections of truth from a x`magic mirror." Gazing at the king from under his brow, a sinister twinkle set his lustrous jade stare aglow. "No voyage is ever simple. No departure promises a return. The answer you seek is a prize you must *earn*."

The king kept his composure, searching the faces of his guests for tips on how he should respond. After a long pause, he settled on the diplomatic approach. "Do you have some guidance or truth to offer that could help us understand this perplexing situation?"

"You think the truth will be easier to understand?" Sterling pondered, clucking his tongue. "What a rudimentary life you must lead."

Clamping his hand over his mouth, Liam beseeched his queen with a look that clearly stated *I'm out of ideas, you try.*

"You know of the truth? Tell me." Sass wafting from her crowned head, to her bejeweled toes, Evelyn sipped from her glass.

"Your wise and wondrous oracle could scour this entire realm for Marooner's Rock until the very end of his days, and he'll never find it," Sterling stated, shooting me an apologetic grimace.

Stomach churning at the fish on my plate, I managed to toss back an indifferent shrug.

After dabbing her lips with her napkin, Queen Evelyn gently laid it onto the linen table cloth. "And why is that?'

"Well, I used to think he was like me. Then, I spent time with him. Now he seems more *swiggity swooty*. Whereas I lean toward the *hannie lannie*." As he spoke each nonsensical term, Sterling shifted from pantomiming a puffed-chest warrior march, to a hands-behind-the-head lounge. "You know what I mean?"

One forearm propped on the table, King Liam shook his head and marveled, "Not one damned time since you arrived."

Sterling kept on as if he hadn't heard him or didn't care. "That world, and this one, are not unlike mighty oaks that have grown side by side from saplings: stretching longer and wider with each passing year, yet never intercepting."

"And you can make them cross?" Evelyn asked, her timbre a melodic bird song.

"Time and space are not palpable clay that can be molded or shaped." Holding one hand before him, Sterling rolled his wrist one way and then the other, his fingers fanning with each fluid motion. "It's more like a river bend; ever changing, ever flowing."

"Yet you know how to travel this mysterious route?" The king forced a polite smile until it was well hidden behind his goblet.

Head listing, Sterling's eyes shimmied side to side. "Show me the map. For I can feel the drumming current of palpable time."

Dabbing the corners of his mouth with his napkin, the king shoved his chair back from the table. "The promise of things to come seems to have spoiled my appetite from this expertly prepared grouper. The map is in my study. Let us see if we can scrounge up a bit of information before the next course."

Wiping his face on his sleeve, Sterling pushed his seat back with an ear-piercing screech. "As you wish, my liege. I ask only that we be back before dessert. I feel a tantrum brewing if I miss it."

"A more than fair proposition." With a nod to his trusted men, Liam led the band from the dining room.

Only Queen Evelyn and myself remained at the elaborate spread.

Delicately wiping her lips, Evelyn's posture drooped. "If we are past the point of pretenses, I'll scoot off to bed. Forcing a fake smile is far more exhausting than it appears." With a polite nod in my direction, the withering-rose queen excused herself.

As I watched her disappear down the hall, a ghostly voice whispered against my ear, "He saw her in every woman. The whispered caress of hair brushing a shoulder blade. The soft curve of an elegant neck. Even in her absence, she haunted him." A swirl of brimstone smoke and Hades appeared in King Liam's seat. "Hey ya, kid. You haven't forgotten about your mermaid honey already, have you? Saw a pretty human and went all moon-eyed? I didn't peg you to be the easily swayed type."

"Don't presume you know *anything* about me," I snarled, fingers curling around the hem of the linen table cloth to prevent me from lunging at the demi-god.

"Oh, I'm sure you're a completely unique mystery." Snagging a grape from the bowl in front of him, Hades popped it in his mouth and talked around each chomp. "You *definitely* aren't enduring this gathering by holding on to the unrealistic hope that *she* will somehow appear. For only your darling Vanessa can brighten a room, and chase away the dark shadows of your heart with her beatific glow. Or that one stolen glance from her could soften the blow of being torn from the only home you've ever known. No, you're right. I know *nothing* about you."

"Why are you here, Hades?" Somehow my butter knife found its way into my white-knuckled grip. The idea of embedding it in his trachea was an intoxicating notion.

"I'm not really here. Only you can see me. Your imagination conjured me out of looming regret over your life choices." Leering at a sinewy blonde handmaid that scurried in to clear the table, Hades shot her a wink. "Hello, my dear. Ever had a little evil in ya? Do you want to?"

"You're vile and smell of rotten eggs," the girl shot back, stalking off with an armload of plates.

Forcing myself to release the polished utensil, I shoved my chair back from the table. "Does any amount of truth *ever* pass your lips?"

Hades' mouth screwed to the side. "How would I know? I can't be expected to pay attention to *everything* I say."

As an angry red haze tinged the edges of my vision, I ground my teeth to the point of pain. "What do you want, Hades?"

Leaning in, the Lord of the Underworld rested his arms on the edge of the mahogany table. "I'm here to finish what the High Priestess started, and make you the augur we need you to be. I'm afraid my method won't be nearly as delicate and lovely as hers." The crystal around his neck pulsating a deep cobalt, Hades' voice dropped to a demanding hiss. "*Videtis et nostis.*"

The mysterious words snagged me like a powerful undertow, dragging me to the depths with their hypnotic pull. Clanging sirens resonated through my mind. One heavy-lidded blink and reality melted away. My eyes opened to a world of blood. Its coppery scent permeated the air, choking down my throat. The hammer of thousands of screams drove nails of anguish into my skull.

A bruised and beaten version of Sterling's face swam before me. Bubbling laughter, closer resembling a sob, shook his shoulders. A reptilian talon held him by the throat. One long claw fish-hooked the corner of his mouth.

Sterling begged.

Pleaded.

Screamed out for mercy as his captor applied steady, unrelenting pressure.

Tissue tore in a series of sickening pops. Gore painted Sterling's neck in torrents.

His scars. This was how he acquired them.

As his eyes rolled back, the world around me spun in a dizzying blur once more.

Queen Evelyn moved on unsteady legs through the square. Catching herself with one hand on the stone wall, she stared down the alley beside her, terror widening her eyes.

A white-hot jolt of pain, then …

Porcelain perfection streaked with blood.

Lips frozen in a silent scream.

Lifeless grey eyes stared daggers of accusation.

Legs crumbling, a terrified howl tore from my chest. The last thing I heard before sinking into the welcome abyss of unconsciousness was Hades' paltry apology. "I am truly sorry, boy. But, you're ready now."

CHAPTER NINE

The moment I came to, I bolted from the castle. Pounding through the square, my feet burned from the ill-fitting shoes that had been forced upon me. Jostled through the crowd, each body I slammed into pierced me with yet another jarring vision. Warning chimes ravaged my brain, threatening to split my skull from the inside out. Sight blurring, I held one arm out in front of me as I forced my way toward the gate.

A spooked horse carriage crash.
Crippling sickness.
Self-inflicted sword wound.
Stomped underfoot by an ogre.
Choked on a chicken bone.
Snake bite.

Thank my frantic state for the guards opening the gate at the sight of me. Only when I burst from the confines of civilization did I expel the breath I hadn't realized I was holding. Hands on my knees, I gulped down lungful after lungful of pine-laced air.

"You, there! Are you well, lad?" a guard atop the wall shouted down.

Terrified he would send someone to check after me and elicit another stabbing prediction, I held up one hand in acknowledgment. Forcing my leaden legs in the direction of the desolate woods, I sought to find a hollowed-out tree stump, or cave where I could hide to ride out this nightmare.

"There's our elusive oracle!" a chiming voice chirped from all around. "Your little vanishing act impressed even me! That's quite a feat."

Spinning around, my stare locked on Sterling. "Stay where you are!" I pleaded. "Don't come down!"

"Don't come …" Sterling trailed off, glancing around in question. Shoulders sagging, one exasperated hand fell off the branch that held him. "I'm in a tree again! *How the blazes does this keep happening?*"

Shrugging off the question as nonessential, he wrapped his arms around himself in a straight jacket hug and rolled to the side. He bent his knees, easily absorbing the shock of his landing. "I'm getting better at that," he mused, brushing the tree bark from his shirt front. "Granted, it's out of necessity, but a welcome improvement still."

Scrambling back, I stumbled over an unearthed tree root and fell to the ground. Acorns and pebbles gouging my palms did nothing to slow my frenzied crab crawl. "Stay back! I beg of you."

Interest sparked silver glints in his wild green eyes. Without a word, he stretched one leg out and pointed a toe in my direction.

"No! *Please!*" I whimpered. Scooting away farther still, my back smacked into a boulder and pinned me there.

"Is this a game?" he chortled, skipping closer like a merry garden sprite. "It's quite enticing!"

Biting the inside of my cheek hard enough to taste blood, I forced the words through my teeth. "*It's not a game. Come no closer.*"

Squatting down, his knees beside his shoulders, Sterling waddled forward with his face folded in worry. "Are you having an episode? Those can be off-putting at first. Would you like to know what works for me?"

Before I could move to stop him, his hand—meant to comfort— caught mine.

Those ear-piercing chimes hurled me into the pit of despair.

Spurting foam tinged with blood. Fur sprouting to the chorus of cracking bone. Pain, the likes of which I never knew existed.

Feeble mind unable to process the onslaught, my eyes rolled back and escaped into darkness.

Groaning, I tried to sit up, only to find it required a Herculean effort.

"I wouldn't attempt movement quite yet, lest you want to empty the contents of your gullet on the floor," a raspy voice suggested, accompanied by clinking bottles and scuffed steps.

"Where am I?" I managed, tongue dry and swollen.

"Back at the castle," King Liam explained, edging into my sight line. "I called upon the High Priestess to aid you. It's the least I could do. This is my fault, and I feel simply dreadful."

"As you should." Pushing past him, the High Priestess set a clay bowl of water on the end table beside me, its contents sloshing out onto the wood. "I warned you of what could happen. Now, this lad gets to pay the price. With all due respect, Your Highness, off with you. Let me tend to him."

"Of course," the king accepted with a nod and moved to the door. "Keep me apprised on his progress. The sooner he can claim that mirror, the sooner we can find a way to remove this affliction."

The moment the door thumped shut behind him, the High Priestess wrung out a rag from within the bowl. "There is no way to remove this burden, don't set your mind to that. I told the king as much before he bid me to invoke it. But a mind determined is hard to sway. The most we can do, is help you to manage it."

I winced as she brought the cloth to my forehead. Muscles contracted and rigid, spittle foamed at the corners of my mouth. Behind my lids, war raged.

The Priestess, locked in magical battle against a dark fae. Bolts of energy, cast from their palms, demolishing the forest in sprays of green and black.

"Just as I suspected." Clucking her tongue against the roof of her mouth, the round-faced woman pulled her hand back. "Your muscles seize when you have an episode. Don't tell me what you saw. That knowledge is not mine to possess. Could you detach yourself from it, I wonder? Did you know it wasn't real?"

Raising one arm, heavy as an iron anchor, I wiped my mouth with the back of my hand. "It looked, smelled, and sounded real. Who was I to argue?"

"Mhmm, mhmm." Grey hair, tucked back in a haphazard bun, waggled as she dipped her head to search her bag of supplies. "We can't have you getting lost in a vision. You're no good to anyone that way. Is there a theme to what you see? And spare the incumbrance of details, please."

"Death … and pain." Giving life to the visions by speaking of them out loud caused bile to scorch up the back of my throat.

"Every time?"

"Exclusively."

"Thought as much," she muttered to herself, dropping a few chosen items onto the dusty mattress with a muffled thump. "More will come, of a less dire lot. An onslaught of information has been forced upon you. Your mind is working tirelessly to decipher it all." Her gnarled, arthritic hands twisted and braided a string of twine. Sizing it to the proper needed length, she broke the unneeded thread with her teeth. "I'm going to have to touch you again. Brace yourself, lad."

"*Mhmm.*" I grimaced, biting back the jolt of her skin brushing mine.

Quickly, the High Priestess worked. Placing a smooth black stone in the center of my palm, she tied it with the braided twine, then looped the three loose ends around my wrist, pinkie finger, and index finger before securing it with a square knot.

"Close your hand around that," she ordered, tone leaving no room for argument.

Obediently, I obliged. The second I enveloped the smooth stone with my touch, a bite of cold potent enough to make the Arctic merfolk shiver shocked through me. "*Mother Ocean's crater crack*! What was that?" Spreading my fingers out wide, I attempted to shake off the lingering effects.

Loosening the ties, the priestess inspected the flesh beneath. "*That* was a stone infused with a lone tear from the Ice Queen.

Sweet girl. *Horrible* to throw surprise parties for. That poor reindeer never saw it coming."

"And what was the point of this experiment?" I asked, gaze fixed on the stone ceiling overhead. "To see if you could make me squeal like a little girl?"

"See that?" she asked, smacking my arm once, and again. "And that? I'm touching you and you're not having a vision. The pain allows you to keep yourself in check. This isn't cruelty, it's control. Feel yourself slipping into a vision, close your hand around that. The shock may not be enough to pull you out of it altogether, but it will remind you of what's real and what's not."

"Thank you," I mumbled, finding the phrase horribly inadequate.

Gathering her scattered supplies, she dropped them unceremoniously into the bag from whence they came. "I only wish I could do more."

Holding my hand up before me, I studied the muted black stone now so crucial to my sanity. "Will this help me find the mirror?"

Brow puckering, the High Priestess' mouth opened, only to have her sentiment cut off by a knock at the door.

"High Priestess Flora, it's Queen Evelyn," her sweet voice trilled from the other side of the heavy wood door. "A thousand apologies for the intrusion. I mean only to check on Alastor's well-being."

Shoving off the edge of my mattress with a huff, the priestess I now knew as Flora padded to the door. "I can't exactly deny access to her royal highness of enchanting perfection," she muttered to herself. Hand curling around the polished brass doorknob, she threw it open and offered a curt nod of respect to the high lady of Caselotti. "Your Majesty."

Head falling back against the pillow, I treated my sleepy eyes to a long blink.

"Flora." Gracing her with a sweet smile, Queen Evelyn handed over a tightly wrapped bundle. "I brought you thistle and poppy from the royal gardens. I remember you used them in quite a few of your salves."

Begrudgingly, Flora's expression softened. I wouldn't say she warmed to her new visitor, but looked slightly less like she had been sucking lemons. "My supply *has* run short, and I'm in need of these. Thank you for not bringing me a completely worthless gift."

A zestful peal of light-hearted laughter bubbled from Evelyn's lips. "Oh, madame, you are such a treat!"

"Wasn't trying to be," Flora mumbled. Cradling the bundle in her arms, she shuffled to her satchel to stow them away.

"And how is our patient doing today?" Evelyn chirped. Folding her hands demurely before her, she floated to the edge of my bed with effortless grace.

I filled my lungs to capacity and opened my eyes in search of a glimmer of divinity from the shimmer that surrounded the queen, even in her ailing state.

My hungry gaze hunted, and found … nothing good or holy.

Even the somber gloom of sickness had vanished. A fiery red blaze cocooned her, veins of commanding black pulsing through it.

Pulse beating an ominous chorus in my temples, beastly unease hatched in my gut and wriggled out a warning. No miraculous healing was to thank for this. Darkness writhed within the queen, cloaked in the skin of an angel.

Closing my hand around my new stone of salvation, I clasped it tight and prayed for release from this fresh hell. Nothing changed. Biting back the pain, I squeezed harder still, barely suppressing the scream choking up the back of my throat.

Blinking her alarm, Evelyn's head tilted. "Alastor? Are you well?"

My lungs scorching with anguish, and it felt as though my gills returned without warning, dooming me to suffocate on dry land.

Salvation came in the form of the High Priestess. Seeing my distress, she shooed the regal queen toward the door. "He wasn't ready for this. I see that now. We need to let him rest, and prepare for his heroic journey ahead."

"Yes, of course." Evelyn forced a tight smile, the extravagant folds of her gown snapping and settling as she strode to the door.

In a moment she would be gone … yet, I had to know.

Forcing my mouth open, the words came rough as gravel. "Your Highness, before I begin my quest, I must know. The advice you gave me before, does it still hold true?"

Evelyn's brow puckered, somehow making her look all the more beguiling. "My mind is often muddled by sickness. If you would be so kind as to remind me?"

The lie souring on my tongue, I spat the words with feigned neutrality, "You told me to retrieve the mirror, no matter the cost."

53

Tipping her head, she granted me an enchanting smile. "That alone is my heart's wish."

Wallowing in grief, I closed my eyes. Could it be? Had the horrific vision I saw already come to pass? Did some form of malevolent darkness now rule the beloved queen?

If so, I had failed her while lying on my back like a barnacle.

Hand closing tight around the stone, I reveled in its burn.

CHAPTER TEN

W here are we off to?" Sterling asked. Perched on the edge of the mattress, his legs crisscrossed beneath him.

Stomping around the room, my bare feet slapped against the cold slate floor. After tucking my dagger into the back of my belted slacks, I flung the cloak he gifted me around my shoulders and thumbed the button into place. "We are useless to these people, and therefore are leaving. Having failed before even beginning, there's no sense in wallowing in their disappointment when they learn their queen is already lost to them."

"Especially with her still walking around and smiling." Sterling blinked my way, head listing as if weighing my lunacy. "That body of logic has no legs under it at all."

"Whether they accept it for truth, or not, doesn't make it any less so." Shoving on one boot, then the other, I stalked for the door.

"I fear you'll hate yourself if you go," Sterling *tsk*ed.

Throwing the door open, I growled through my teeth, "I'm prepared to live with that."

"I'm not," Sterling trilled, letting one shoulder rise and fall in a casual shrug.

I blinked, and the world shifted. Staggering back to reclaim my faltering footing, my back smacked into the far wall of the bedroom. My boots were back off, cloak slung over the chair, dagger sitting on the bureau where I claimed it. The door was clasped shut once more, taunting me with the promise of eluding escape.

"I'm right back where we started from! What did you do?"

"I put you back where we started from. You just said that. You should listen when you talk." Popping to his feet, Sterling shook out his legs.

"*Don't* do it again," I warned, collecting my belongings a second time.

"That directive is a bit unclear." Sterling tapped at his chin with the tip of one finger. "What is the *it* you refer to? Follow you? Speak to you? Or, perhaps, you meant this?"

Another hiccup of time and that stone wall was snagging the fabric of my shirt yet again.

"*How are you doing this, you infuriating little imp?*" I bellowed, face reddening with rage. "Plus, what business is it of yours if I stay or go? These people tried to lock you in the stocks upon your first meeting. Do you claim to care for them?"

Lacing his fingers, Sterling stretched his arms over his head and yawned. "Make me sound cold and heartless if you like. *I'm* not the one condemning the queen to a death sentence."

"The good in her has already died." That ugly truth weighted my bones with defeat, sagging my posture. "There's nothing left to save."

"My how life has jaded you." Sterling curled around me with feline fluidity, his gaze scouring my face as if searching for a thread to unravel. "Have you thought at all of Princess Snow? Don't we owe it to her to at least *attempt* to save her mother? Terrible things can befall a child not raised by a loving hand."

Dragging one palm over my weary eyes, I said a silent prayer for clarity. "I didn't realize you were such an advocate to the cause."

Forehead rippled with confusion, Sterling pulled back. "Cause? Or did you say claws? Is there a monster afoot?" A shudder rippled through him, and lucidity once again sharpened his foggy stare. "Oh, yes! Quick now. I feel this reality is fading away. Concentration through limerick should allow it to stay. I have a proposition, good for us as it is for the baby. A mission for answers, and long-awaited prophecy, maybe. We could set off for adventure, just as we planned. Brave and bold lads, following the king's command. Along the way, we each use the mirror to find our own truth. I have many questions and find myself a piss-poor sleuth. After that, we give the king his prize, and the path of our future will be ours to decide. I will finally return to the family I miss, while you can swim home to that deep-sea abyss."

"Why ... are you speaking in rhymes?" I couldn't help but ask.

"What can I say," he replied with a pained grimace, "it passes the time."

Retrieving my dagger from the bureau, he flipped it over and offered it to me by the hilt. "Can we venture on together as partners chasing destiny? Or shall I continue looping time until you're as mad as me?"

As I accepted the blade, I found myself softening to the strange little man.

"Tonight, we rest. Tomorrow," hitching one brow, I borrowed his melodic cadence, "on to the quest."

CHAPTER ELEVEN

U nable to sleep, I paced the length of my room long after the moon rose to its highest glory. Passing the line of preparedness, I crossed straight into obsessive territory as I checked my satchel of supplies time and again. Food, water, clothing, map, weapons, an enchanted artifact that prevented me from being sucked into a hallucination and lost forever—you know, camping essentials. I couldn't help but think I would feel more confident if I had *any* idea where I was going. Unfortunately, King Liam and his men whispered behind closed doors with Sterling over that. Something he had said had convinced the king he could get us to Marooner's Rock. Sterling. The guy who found himself in trees with no recollection of how or why. There was a good chance he would be the death of me.

It was on yet another pass of the mirror when a strobing blue light from within beckoned me to it. Edging closer, my own lost and confused reflection was nowhere to be seen. In its place, watery diamonds danced and shifted in an enchanting light show orchestrated by the demands of the current. Sea gulls cawed. The tide crashed against a far-off shore. My feet stumbled closer, drawn to the glimpse of home.

Catching the side of the mirror, I leaned in as a figure appeared in the distance. Raven hair danced around enchanting features. An amethyst tail swiveled side to side with effortless grace.

Unable to blink or exhale, I gawked at the impossible. "Vanessa?"

As she neared, her hand rose in front of her, out-stretched fingers calling to me. Trembling, I matched the motion. I expected the cold nothingness of glass. Instead, my heart lurched in a stutter-beat when my fingers sank into rippling water. Energy crackled between us, the tips of her fingers floating to mine. Gills, running along the bottom of her rib cage, clamped shut in breathless anticipation.

Time stopped.

Reality bent to our will.

Flesh found flesh. Tentative at first, not believing such a miracle to be possible. Urgency and insistence growing, our fingers laced together and held firm. Pulling against my hand, Vanessa drew herself to me, my name forming on her heart-shaped lips.

Her arm followed mine out, the moonlight glimmering off her sandstone skin. Heart hammering, I watched her thick lashes brush the tops of her cheeks as she closed her eyes and crossed the barrier into the unknown.

Fins were replaced by a shimmering gown of onyx and plum. An intoxicating smile warmed her features.

I feared blinking, that such an ordinary act may chase this heavenly mirage away. Bringing her hand to my mouth, I dotted a kiss to her palm and breathed in her scent—the crisp, clean breeze after a summer storm.

"Once again I'm astounded by your power. I never should have doubted you would find me," I murmured against her velvet skin.

"Yet you did?" The sweet cadence of her voice soothed my troubled soul.

Weaving my fingers into her hair, I tipped her lips to mine. I hesitated, savoring the warmth of her breath on my face. "I am a silly, stupid man. And I will *never* make that mistake again."

White hot need blossomed in my core. Unable to hold back a minute longer, I crushed my mouth to hers.

Sulfur.

Death.

Wailing agony.

My eyes snapped open.

Pulling back, I searched her face with the locked-on intensity of a shark smelling blood. "I haven't been this happy since we laid in the red Caboma fields behind the castle together."

A rosy blush crept up her neck and kissed her cheeks pink. "You held me close and we daydreamed about the day we would rule the kingdom together. A moment, precious as a bubble, viciously popped by time and circumstance."

"I could say the same for your charm and influence." Ice seeped into my tone. Hand snaking up, I closed my grip around her throat to plant her there.

Fingernails scraping at my arm, she clawed for freedom. "Alastor, what are you doing?" The words escaped her in a panicked wheeze.

"Funny thing about Caboma, it's a fresh water plant," I rumbled through my teeth. "It couldn't be sustained anywhere near the salty depths of Atlantica. *All* merfolk know that. Which poses the question; *who are you?*"

Mischievous glee crinkled the corners of her eyes, a mocking smile curling up the corners of her mouth. "Can't blame us for trying, gorgeous. We were swimming off for our happily ever after for a moment there."

Releasing her, I took a wide step back. Goose flesh shivering down my arms. "You referred to yourself in plural form."

"Shame that you put all of this together before things got really fun." As she spoke, Vanessa's voice became a chorus of varying octaves and timbres. In an image that threatened to haunt me forever, my love's face smoothed to a flat, inhuman canvas. Skin rippled. Flaps of flesh curled open. Two eyes morphed to six. The air shimmered, three distinct shapes squirmed from the confines of Vanessa's form. Rolling and stretching, they grew, adapting their own characteristics as they right themselves.

"*Siren! Speak no more!*" Recognizing the three-headed beast from the courtyard—because such a thing would be hard to forget—I overturned the table in my frantic scramble for distance.

"Siren?" Two hitched one brow, her full lips pursed into a pout. "Because a creature of our distinction couldn't *possibly* have a name? How would you like it if we called you Undistinguishable Merman Destined to Die on His Quest? Stings a bit, doesn't it?"

"Easy, sister. Such a sweet, tasty morsel couldn't possibly have meant any harm. He needs to be nurtured … *educated*." Something in the way Three enunciated the word *educated* made it sound naughty, and dripping with hedonistic intent. "Our name is Cerberus, dear one. We would *love* to hear how it rolls from your tongue. Particularly in between breathless pants."

Annoyed by her sister's antics, One shriveled her with a sideways glare. "On behalf of those that share all lower extremities with you … no we wouldn't, and stop it."

"What do you want?" Hand hovering at my hip, my fingers twitched for the dagger.

"Simply to deliver a message from our master," all three purred in unison, which somehow made it all the more off-putting.

"Hades," I hissed.

Stalking a slow circle around me, their wandering stares traveled over every inch of my body. "You may thank him when you hear what we have to say."

"Doubtful," I countered. "I want as little to do with Hades and his wretched minions as possible."

Three cocked her head, azure eyes narrowing to slits. "Didn't you swear allegiance to him? Shall we welcome you to the wretched family?"

"Sister, don't taunt him," Two chastised, amusement playing across her features. "Not when *his master* has such big plans for him." Chuckling at how I bristled, she pressed on. "First, a warning. When the High Priestess awoke the oracle essence, another was unleashed as well."

"The trickster," I breathed, recalling the High Priestess' warning to King Liam.

"Such a good boy, paying attention," One mockingly cooed.

"Indeed, the trickster. Its spirit has yet to find a host. Perhaps you've sensed it?" Coiling around me, Two's mouth brushed my ear. "A shiver up your spine? Disembodied giggle echoing down a hall? That's him."

I pulled away, my nose crinkling in disgust. "What does that have to do with me? I'm previously possessed and up to occupancy, thanks to your proprietor."

"Without guidance, the trickster will pick its own vessel. And, with that naughty little spirit, you can trust it to be drawn to the truly wicked." Finishing yet another prowled circle, Cerberus planted their feet directly in front of me and spoke through all three heads. "That's where you come in. A darkness has come to Kingdom Caselotti. One hungry for power and vengeance. If it becomes host to the mischievous Menehune essence, it will wield the accompanying powers in malevolent ways you cannot begin to comprehend."

I hooked my thumbs in the waist of my slacks and feigned indifference. "How is any of that my problem?"

Stepping in, body-skimming close, the three heads swayed mere inches from my face. "Because, we believe you've encountered this particular dark entity before, Alastor. And it would take great pleasure in ensuring you never make it back to the ocean."

I cast my stare out the window, gazing out at the freedom eluding me more and more with each passing day. "What would you have me do?" I reluctantly spat.

Patting my chest with their shared hand, Three purred, "There's a good lad. You merely need to direct the essence into a proper host. One sweet, and good, and an endearing degree of ... mad."

Head snapping around, I shifted my stare from one haunting face to the next in search of answers. "Sterling? No! I couldn't! He's barely holding himself together as is!"

One's eyebrows lifted to her hairline, lips twisting into an ironic smirk. "The fact that you instantly knew who we were talking about should say something about your choice in friends."

"Silence!" Two barked at her sister, lip curling into a snarl. The chastisement lasted only a beat, after which she blinked my way with a soft, welcoming smile fixed into place. "The Menehune will not harm him, only bolster what he already has. It could prove to be of great benefit to him. *If*, someone cares enough to keep a vigil watch and guide him."

"Why would I do that to him?"

"Preventative measures." Cerberus lifted one shoulder in a nonchalant shrug, Two speaking for them all. "Elsewise, your path back to your princess could be destroyed. All you have to do is string this totem around your odd little friend's neck. It will draw the essence right to him. A simple act, to help clear your path home."

Dangling from their middle finger, the totem swung between us. No more than an inch tall, the hand-carved wood ornament looked like some sort of primate. "And this won't hurt him?"

My hand raised as if moving of its own accord, allowing the three-headed creature to settle the artifact into my outstretched palm. "Not if you're there to help him," they coaxed in perfect harmony.

Pulse pounding in my temples, I watched my hand curl around the necklace in stunned disbelief. I couldn't actually be considering this, could I?

"Oh, and, Alastor?" Jolted from my reverie, I glanced up to find the Cerberus back in the mirror, the Underworld now smoldering around them. "We'll be waiting the moment you return with the mirror. Don't fall victim to the mistaken notion you could slink off with it undetected."

Turning their back to me, they trudged on—ash coating the ground beneath their feet ignited to smoldering embers with each step. The black cloak fastened around their shoulders snapped and lashed behind them like a living whip, warning the living and deceased of the power bestowed on them by the master of death.

CHAPTER TWELVE

I loathed myself for considering it. Yet there I was, tiptoeing down the hall with lantern in hand. I rationalized that I would see him through whatever came of this, that I would remain firmly by his side until we could *both* find a way out from under the burden of these afflictions. Even so, the whispering voice of my conscious knew otherwise. If I did this, it was for no other reason than fear of losing any chance of returning to Vanessa. How did Sterling play into that return to the depths? I didn't know, and that's the part that made me a selfish ass.

Even as I raised my fist to rap on his door, I wrestled with the decision. I would be cursing a tortured soul that deserved kindness and mercy. What kind of monster would that make me? "Sterling? You awake?"

"Hmm? Alastor?" his murmured response came muffled through the door. "Come on in."

Swallowing hard, I opened the door, all the while praying the right answer would magically reveal itself. What I found, instead, was a vacant room. "Uh, Sterling? There's no trees in here, therefore I'm out of places to look. Where are you?"

"Where am I? That's a very good question. *Ow!*" A thump shook his bed, followed by another. "Oh. Oh, no. *I–I think I'm buried alive! Alastor! Help me!*" He kicked and flailed until squirming out from under the bed frame. The instant he saw light, his shrieks died on his lips. "Nope! Just got stuck under the bed again. What can I help you with?"

"I, uh, just wondered if you and the king had discovered a route for our journey tomorrow?" I lied, fiddling with the totem dangling from my wrist.

Springing to his feet, Sterling shook off the dust bunnies covering him. "In a matter of speaking. He showed me the map. It's not a land I've ever traveled to before. Even so, I believe, if we can gather a crew to mediate on that exact location, I may be able to ride their waves and get us there." As he spoke, his jade stare fixated on the totem, watching it bob and swivel. "What is that? I want it."

Taken aback by his interest, I peered down at the little wooden monkey charm dangling from the heel of my hand. "This is ..." For the life of me, I couldn't come up with one good lie. With a clearer head I may have taken that as the answer I so desperately sought.

"A gift?" Sterling perked. "For me?"

"Do you want it?" I asked, raising the bauble for him to get a better look.

Eyes narrowing, he tilted his head in inspection. "I ... feel like it already belongs to me."

It couldn't be that easy, could it? Just let him claim what he wants, thereby removing all guilt? No. I couldn't do that to a being so in need of someone to look out for him.

"I brought this for you, actually," I admitted, pulling my hand back. "But I'm not sure this is a gift you're going to want."

"I can tell you with utmost certainty that I do," Sterling countered, reaching around me to swipe at it.

Ducking out of reach, I attempted to inject rational thought into his frenzy. "Sterling, I need you to listen to me. This totem has an enchantment on it. If you put this on it will call a spirit to you that will amplify all your— what do you call them? —*jumping* abilities ten-fold."

Crest-fallen, Sterling's crumpling features tugged from the treasure to search my face. "And ... you want that of me? More of these oddities?"

"Not if you don't want them," I admitted, finally finding the strength to speak from my heart. "If you feel it calls to you, and you welcome the added power it will supply, I will tie it around your neck and be here for you no matter what follows. But, if you have any hesitation at all, we will throw it into the fire together and let that essence select its own host. Come what may."

"The added power, it's real?" Sterling appeared more startled child than man, his eyes bulging with trepidation.

"It is." Pulling the string, I untied the Menehune charm from my wrist. "It has a counterpoint, the oracle, which I was infected with. The two sides are said to keep each other in balance ... or something along those lines. The details I've gotten have been a bit sketchy. I *can* say that since that fun little nuance came into my life, I'm regularly subjected to nightmarish visions that will haunt me the remainder of my days."

"Or, as I call that, any given day," Sterling stated with a heavy slathering of grief.

Feeling guilty for having brought it up at all, I stepped back and hid the totem behind my leg. "You know what, you need not worry of such things. With everything you're already forced to endure—"

"*Heightened abilities might help me find my way back to my Alice!*" Sterling erupted. The idea sparked a fresh light behind his eyes, illuminating his face with giddy enthusiasm. "Yes! Oh, yes! This is brilliant! Quick, now! Let's have it!"

"Who's Alice?" I asked, shrinking away from his frantic grabby hands.

"She's my Alice, of course!" He snorted, as if that was the most ludicrous question he had ever heard. Seizing my shoulder, he shoved me aside and snatched the totem from my grip. "First thing in the morning, we will gather the king's best men to help guide our jump to Marooner's Rock. Once we do, we will grab that mirror, and deliver it to the forever-grateful king. Then, thanks to this charm, I may finally be able to go home!"

"Don't you think you're getting ahead of yourself a tad?" My query was interrupted by Sterling slapping at my hand and gesturing for me to tie the trinket around his neck. Rolling my eyes, I reluctantly obliged. "You said yourself that finding the exact location could take a while."

A soft knock rattled the door before Sterling could answer. "Sir, is everything okay?"

"Yes, everything is fine. Now go away," Sterling shouted. Arranging the talisman in the center of his breast bone, he threw his arms out wide and closed his eyes.

Nothing.

Not even a breeze stirred.

"Well," clapping my hands in front of me, I rubbed my palms together, "this looks like it could be a rather lengthy process. I'll go grab a pillow and blanket from my—" I turned around and the words died on my lips.

His bed chamber was gone, replaced by a lush green jungle. On a fallen log a mere arm's distance away, a fat frog croaked his welcome. Head whipping in one direction then the other, I gaped in disbelief. "*Sterling, what have you done?*"

Hands slapping to his sides, he spun, marveling at the change in scenery. "I … think it's Marooner's Rock. I wager if we walk west we'll find a cove with a giant boulder in the center, and venturing east should be a lagoon. All I did was think of it, and here we are. If I knew it would be that easy, I would have left a note before vanishing without a trace."

"*Help, please!*" a soft voice yelped.

Posture straightening, Sterling's voice dropped to an urgent whisper. "I think I'm hearing voices now. Is that part of it? Hearing things?"

"That's not in your head, that's a child in trouble!" I exclaimed, darting in the direction of the plea.

Leaves crunching underfoot, I charged through the unfamiliar landscape. Pushing aside a massive palm frond, my toes skidded to a stop at the edge of a cliff. Rocks rained down on the chestnut-eyed child staring up at me. His fingers curled over the rocky ledge were all that prevented him from plummeting to a fatal conclusion.

Dropping to my knees, I grasped his forearm. "I've got you," I assured him, "pull yourself up."

Feet scraping against the stone wall, the frightened lad fought his way up. Collapsing onto his hands and knees, his breath came in ragged pants. As he blinked up at me, his thick lashes brushed the tops of freckled covered cheeks. Ruffled russet strands darted from his head, falling haphazardly across his forehead. Tucked into a small satchel at his hip hung a wooden pan flute.

Wetting his parched lips, he wheezed, "The walls … they vanished."

Recognizing his voice caused an icy bucket of awareness to slosh over me. "You work in the palace? Were you the one who knocked on the door?"

"Aye, I saw a light on in one of the chambers and wanted to see if all was well," he admitted, chin falling to his chest. "His Highness took me in after my papa died, and I want to prove myself a hard, and loyal worker."

Hopping up on a nearby boulder, Sterling craned his neck to inspect this strange new world. "Seems there's a lesson in there somewhere about the importance of minding one's business," he mused. "Not that I ever adhered to it."

"Will you be quiet," I hissed over my shoulder. Crouching down, I dipped to eye level with the boy. "Peter, is that your name?"

"N–no." He shook his head, brow furrowed in confusion.

"Your flute," my chin jerked in the direction of the instrument, "P. T. R. is carved on it."

"Those are my initials." Pushing off his knuckles, he sat back on his knees in the grass. "Phineas Theodore Rutherford. People call me Phin for short."

"A name I can appreciate," I stated, and offered him my hand. "It's a pleasure to meet you, Phin. My name is Alastor, and this wild-eyed fella is Sterling."

"I know who you are." Shaking my hand, a tentative smile tugged at his lips. "You're the champions that are going to save the queen."

Arms thrown back, wind whipped through young Phin's hair as he sailed over the treetops.

Shaking off the hold of my first pleasant vision with surprising ease, I dropped his hand and rose to full height. "That is why we're here," I muttered, my lack of conviction audible even to my own ears. Hand still linked with that of the freckle-faced lad, I helped him to his feet. "You, on the other hand, need to get back to the castle before the king misses you. Sterling, could you help our new friend with that?"

Arms swinging limp at his sides, Sterling's mouth sagged into a frown. "No."

The absurdity of the situation forced a nervous laugh to bubble from my chest. "You say that in jest, of course? This is one of your jokes I just don't get?"

"No, I ... wait, you don't get my jokes?"

"Exactly never. Can we focus please?" It was getting increasingly difficult to keep my fake smile fixed for the boy's benefit.

"Seems a rather rude comment to ignore." Muttering to himself, Sterling folded his arms over his chest and stepped off his rock pedestal. "As I was saying, regretfully, I cannot simply whisk the boy back. *I* am the vessel. The vessel is me. It hops from here to there, but seldom in the same spot twice. One or two venture back, the third becomes a victim of time and space with no guaranteed return."

Mouth swinging open, I could form no more eloquent response than, "W–what?"

"We jump together when the job is complete, or we don't jump at all. Because I can't guarantee I can find my way back to this exact time and space again," Sterling explained with a clarity and resolve uncharacteristic of him.

Tugging on the bottom hem of my shirt, Phin peered up at me. "Both me mum and dad have gone to be with the Lord. There isn't a soul in Caselotti that will even notice I'm gone. It would be my honor to travel with the Queen's Champions, sir."

My heart bled compassion and understanding for the boy tossed here and there by the current of circumstance, same as me. "I know that feeling all too well."

Offering me a toothy smile, Phin's face told the story of a child hungering for love and acceptance. "Does that mean I can embark on this adventure with you?"

While I couldn't in good conscious put his life in unnecessary risk, I failed to see what choice I had. In place of a response, I stepped to the edge of the cliff I had plucked him from and gazed out at the ocean of emerald greenery. I had no idea what lay ahead, but I put my trust in Mother Ocean that she had thrown this wayward team together for a reason.

"Welcome to Marooner's Rock, lads," I boomed, chin tipped toward the horizon. "Right or wrong, from this point on, we're in this together."

CHAPTER THIRTEEN

A purgatory of green cursed with deafening silence. That is the only way I could think to describe the strange new realm I found myself in. Using my dagger to slice through the vining foliage, no disturbed critters scampered away. No roosted birds took to flight. Not one insect buzzed my ears. Even the leaves seemed to dangle still on their branches.

Nothing.

The sound of our clumsy footfalls marked us as interlopers in the forest of stillness. Far too soon, the weight of that smothering silence became unbearable. Every stick that crunched underfoot echoed through the valley like a gunshot. Muscles set on edge, I tensed for an attack I feared lurked somewhere among the trees.

Sun moving slow across the cloudless sky, the hike began to wear on my traveling companions same as me. Phin wrung his wood flute between his hands, gripping it tight to his chest. The farther we ventured into the catacombs of vegetation, the closer he clung to my side. His earlier valor stolen by anxiety.

Then, there was Sterling. Quiet had truly unfortunate side effects on him. In a steady stream of babbling, he adopted varying voices to speak for all the characters rattling through his mind. *"I don't like the looks of it. However, it may kiss my hand if it likes.* I'd rather not, actually." Plucking a long palm frond from a low hanging branch, he pushed his thumb through it to make eye holes, then tied it around his head like a mask. "I wouldn't mind freeing your head from your shoulders and mounting it to my staff. *But, then who would sing the birthday song?* Oh! I do so love a celebration, and the candles!"

Beads of sweat trickling down from between my shoulder blades, I threw a bit more aggression into hacking and sawing my way through the brush. "I have an idea," I grunted between strikes, "how about a bit of conversation to put us *all* at ease? Sterling, what shall we talk about?"

Head tilting at the question, his agitated stare shifted to eerily manic. "*Begin at the beginning, and go on 'til you come to the end. Then, stop.*"

"Well put," I said with a curt nod, and lobbed the conversation to our youngest traveler. "How about you, Phin? Any topics come to mind?"

"Is … is it true?" he ventured, voice quaking with nerves. "That you were once a merman?"

Comforted by thoughts of home, I cast him an appreciative smile. "I didn't realize that matter was one for debate."

"I meant no insult, sir!" Tripping over a tree root, Phin stumbled to reclaim his footing mid-plea. "The women in the kitchen of the castle cluck about all sorts of nonsense. I know better than to listen."

Pausing, I wiped the sweat from my brow with the back of my forearm. "Not nonsense at all. I am … or, *was* a mer, and in my heart forever will be."

"That's amazing!" Phin gushed. Shoulders rising to his ears, he seemed moments from exploding with infinite questions. "What's it like to live … under the sea?"

Falling back into a rhythm with my swings, my heart warmed as I let my thoughts dive to the depths. "I can't say the colors there are any brighter than on land. Yet, against the cobalt cloak of the glittering waves the different shades come alive. Yellow fish glow like rays of the sun. Pink coral sprouts a brighter spectrum than any rose could hope to bloom. And the sound—*oh, the sound!*" Chuckling to myself, I clasped a fist over my heart. "Every night a symphony of lapping waves lulls you to sleep. And, the rushing current provides the comforting chorus of a mother's drumming heart to ease the demands of everyday life." The memories were so vivid in my mind, I could practically hear the crashing waves.

"Where shall we keep the biscuits!" Sterling suddenly yelped.

"It sounds most magical, sir." Whimsy danced through Phin's declaration, both of us choosing to overlook Sterling's babbling. "Did you have a special someone there?"

"Indeed, I did," I stated, the anguish of being torn from Vanessa stabbed into my heart and ground deep.

Noticing my melancholy, Phin hesitated before asking, "When is the last time you spoke to her?"

Closing my eyes, I journeyed back to the last conversation we had outside the mess hall of the Royal Guard training academy. "I ducked beneath a canopy of reeds to find a mesmerizing princess waiting for me. My commanding officer scowled his disdain at such a lowly soldier being visited by a member of the royal family, but Vanessa shriveled him with her regal glare. At the time I remember being annoyed at her for … something. Whatever pointless grievance it was, vanished the instant she turned to me with a smile as inviting as twilight on a white sand beach. I remember holding her. Plucking a driftwood twig from her hair and shaking the strands out in an onyx waterfall. The last thing she said to me was a royal command I fear I can never keep, *'Come back to me, Alastor, and bring forever with you'*."

Needing a distraction from the aching hole in my heart, I resumed swiping a path with renewed vigor.

"Uh, Alastor?" Phin called from a few paces back.

"Is it bath day? *I've forgotten the lavender soap!*" Sterling added, his shrill tone becoming increasingly frantic and unhinged.

"Have to keep moving, lads," I puffed, sweat streaming down my back. "The only way out of this, is through it."

Planting himself firm, Phin insisted, "Alastor, stop. You *really* need to see this."

Filling my lungs, I turned for no other reason than to humor him. Eyes bulging with shock, I momentarily forgot how to exhale. From the hillside we had been hiking around a gorgeous waterfall now flowed. It emptied into a lagoon that had most certainly *not* been there a moment ago. In the center, a scattering of boulders jutted from the water. Seated upon them, a pair of mermaids sunned themselves, their tails rising and falling in casual slaps against the bubbling water. A third paddled circles around them, her arms rising and falling in a lackadaisical back stroke.

"W–where d–did all of this c–come from?" I stammered, struggling to form words.

"As you were talking, things just … appeared!" Throwing his arms out wide, Phin spun in a circle, giggling. *"Do you know what this means?"*

"Not even marginally," I admitted, unable to tear my unblinking stare from the newly formed oasis.

"You thought it, and it materialized!" Breathless from twirling, Phin skittered to a stop. Dizzy and swaying, he dropped his voice to a stage whisper. *"Sir Alastor, you have magic here."*

Sterling threw his hands up in exasperation. "That's what I've been trying to tell you! No one listens to me."

Tucking my dagger in my waistband, I inched closer to the shoreline. "This can't be. It's impossible."

Catching a blade of blue grass, Phin twined it around his finger. "It's easy enough to prove. Think of something else, see if it appears. I know! You're new to the human world. Think of one thing you like about it."

"Oh! I really like those fluttery things. What are they called?" Lifting my shoulders, I flapped my arms. "The brightly colored insects that children terrorize by catching in nets?"

Phin opened his mouth only to clamp it shut again. "I think you mean butterflies. Saying it like that makes me feel horrible for ever having enjoyed chasing them."

"Yes! Butterflies!" No sooner did the words leave my lips, then I felt the air stir. A whispered caress brushed my shoulder, wings rivaling a pelican's in size flapping passed.

The monstrous butterfly zipped around Sterling in a tight circle, making it necessary for him to bend backwards to avoid being slapped in the face by its impressive wingspan.

Dragging a hand over the scruff of my jawline, I mumbled in disbelief, "Was that me? Did I actually make that?"

Dropping to his knees, Phin dragged one hand over the surface of the lagoon. "I think so."

With a flabbergasted shake of my head, I watched Sterling dip, dodge, and shimmy away from the hovering bug that seemed to have taken a keen interest in him. With each flap, the butterfly's wings changed color. Sapphire lined with opalescent ivory. Onyx highlighted by golden amber. Blush pink accented by flashes of plum. Somehow, each pairing managed to be lovelier than the last.

"Reminds me of Queen Amphrite," I muttered to myself, kneeling down in the grass alongside Phin.

"Who's that?" the boy asked, chuckling at Sterling's flailing arms and wild dance moves to dodge the butterfly's advances.

"She was the queen … the *second* queen," I corrected, unable to replace Queen Titonus in my mind even after all this time, "of Poseidon, King of Atlantica and ruler of the Seven Seas. Amphrite had great magic, and enjoyed using it to completely alter her look every time she made any kind of public appearance. One day she would be a willowy blonde, the next a stern brunette. Her own husband could seldom recognize her."

One corner of Phin's mouth screwed to the side in contemplation. "A good queen shouldn't be judged by her appearance in any regard, as long as she is noble and just. Was she that?"

"No. Her beautiful disguises masked a darkened heart. I hate to think of what has become of …" Vanessa's name caught on my lips. No. I had to believe she was okay, because there wasn't a damned thing I could do elsewise, and that knife of despair cut far too deep. Instead, I opted for a less gutting alternative. "… *Atlantica* if Amphrite has found her way back into power. I doubt the kingdom would even resemble the home I once knew."

Wings slapping the air, the butterfly banked hard and dove for Sterling's head. Extending its long, tubular mouth, saliva dripping fangs snapped at the end of the threatening appendage. Sterling's muffled screams came from behind midnight black wings that suction-cupped to his face.

Dagger hissing free at my hip, I leapt to my feet. Before I could throw myself into the melee, Sterling ripped the creature off him and spiked it to the ground. It slammed into a rock with a sickening squish, limp wings draining ashen.

"You killed it," I grimaced, stating the oozing obvious.

Hair shooting off his head in every conceivable direction, brilliant red scratches marred Sterling's cheeks and the bridge of his nose. "How … did you turn that lovely — if not slightly bothersome — creature into a blood thirsty harbinger of death?"

Shoulders lifting to my ears, I shook my head.

"He was talking about the bad queen," Phin interjected, handing Sterling his handkerchief to wipe away the blood.

Dabbing at his wounds, Sterling winced, sucking air through his teeth. "Your thoughts went dark then that same darkness leeched onto my face. While we're here, you need to keep your thoughts light and airy. Because, I've seen the flip side of your brain, pal, and it is *terrifying!*"

"Maybe they just have a hellacious bug problem here?" I offered, hearing that for the pathetic excuse it was.

Stepping close enough for his chest to bump mine, a disheveled Sterling enunciated each word. "*Think. Happy. Thoughts.*"

"With that tone, how could I not?" As if manifested by the mere mention of my happiness, an amethyst tail broke the lagoon's surface with a gentle splash. The color demanding my attention, I moved with a magnetic pull toward the ripples dancing over the water.

Side-stepping in front of me, Sterling's eyes narrowed. "Where are you off to? We need to discuss how to keep you Zen, pally."

Back to me, she rose from the water. Raven hair clung to her shoulders and back like a second skin. Sensing the burning sizzle of my stare, her chin tipped in my direction, gracing me with a glimpse of a profile I had long since memorized. It couldn't be her. Not for real. Even so, the vision made blood sing through my veins, my heart lurching in a spastic stutter-beat.

Grabbing Sterling by his narrow shoulders, I lifted him from the ground and set him down beside me. He uttered a colorful expletive I didn't pretend to hear, my focus drawing me to her like a moth to a candle's flame.

At the snap of a twig under my boot, she turned to me. My fantasy. My beating heart, blinked back at me with purple eyes more rare and treasured than any precious stone. Water lapping at the toes of my boots, I crouched down with one knee in the damp soil. A stroke of her tail and she was close enough for me to see the cluster of three small birthmarks on her left cheek.

"Vanessa." I breathed her name in a wistful exhale.

Giggling, she sank into the water, leaving only her eyes visible.

That's where I found the difference. She was Vanessa, down to every detail. Except for the absence of the rebellious spark that radiated from the stare of the real thing in brilliant silver starbursts.

Deflated by the twisted reality, my other knee sank to the ground. "You're not her."

Pressing her palms to the shore on either side of me, the imposter hoisted her upper body out of the water. Droplets clung to her flesh, dripping from her like diamonds.

"Does it matter?" she murmured, lips teasing over mine.

From behind me came a yelp, followed by the ruckus of a heavy object being dragged.

I wanted to investigate, knew that I should …

One arm snaked around my neck, and the tip of her tongue traced over my lower lip. "Indulge in the illusion," she coaxed in a voice that perfectly replicated Vanessa's. "Succumb to temptation. Either way, you're never leaving this never-land."

Spell broken, I pulled back and caught her wandering hand. "*What?*"

"You'll see," she warned with a malicious chuckle. Yanking free of my hold, she threw herself back in a reverse swan dive, water spraying me in her descent.

Heavy footfalls trudged up behind me, and I rose to my feet in anticipation of a barrage of questions from Sterling and Phin. Instead, I gawked at a looming figure pulling back a boulder-sized fist.

"You never should have come." That sentiment hanging in the air, my face exploded in throbbing pain. A hazy beat later, the ground rose to meet me.

CHAPTER FOURTEEN

A black sack was yanked off my head, leaving me squinting into the blinding daylight. Forced onto my knees, my wrists had been bound behind me. The skin beneath the restricting ties was already chaffed raw.

From beside me, a child's frightened whimper snapped my head in Phin's direction. Tied in the same fashion I was, yet thankfully free of a hood, the lad chanted to himself. "In the darkness of life, hold honor's truth until morning. In the darkness of life, hold honor's truth until morning." Tears streaked down his cheeks, watering the earth in heavy drops.

"Phin." Scooching closer, I offered the only comfort I could— nearness. "Are you okay? Have they hurt you?"

Forcing his gaze to meet mine, his stare begged for a miracle I was impotent to supply. "In the darkness of life, hold honor's truth until morning."

"Curiouser and curiouser, isn't it?"

At the sound of Sterling's voice, my head swiveled. That simple motion caused a wave of vertigo to slam into me, the clearing we were trapped in whirling around me.

Oblivious to my dilemma, Sterling ventured on. "I think his clock gears have slipped. There's a tick, but he's lost his tock."

A team of men milled behind us. They talked in hushed tones, occasionally casting menacing stares in our direction. If these were pirates or bandits, they were unlike any I had ever seen. No garish garb or medallions from their travels decorated the crew's drab clothing. Each was clad in a sandstone pallet of loose fitting shirts and russet pants. Increasingly odd was the fact that not one among them had a sword fastened to their hips. In fact, upon sweeping glance, I saw no weaponry at all. This was no normal gang of rapscallions. A fact which somehow set my nerves further on edge.

"Eyes forward!" a gruff voice barked at the men.

Without hesitation they snapped to attention.

"I fear we could be here forever." Sterling chewed on his lower lip, shifting his weight from one knee to the other. "But sometimes forever only lasts a second."

A choked sob tore from Phin's throat, fat tears streaming down his freckle smattered cheeks.

"We will get through this." Jaw squared, I fixed my stare straight ahead, unwilling to entertain any other alternatives. "Of that I have no doubt."

A sudden silence fell over the clearing, festering with the same deadly intent of a readied cannon.

"Where did you find them?" The question was posed by a female—her tone satin smooth, with the same threat to devour as a Great White's jaws.

"In the valley," came the humble response.

"They made a mermaid lagoon," another tagged on.

Heat rushed through my core at the memory of Vanessa's body skimming mine.

No, not Vanessa. One that could never be her.

Stalking a slow circle around us, the yet to be seen woman scuffed the heel of her boots as she walked. "A flock of birds of the most *extraordinary* colors flew over my head during my trek here. I assume they are to blame for that as well?"

"Yes, Sergeant," her men obediently chorused.

Voice sharpening to a dagger's edge, she spun on her heel toward her trembling troops. "*I shouldn't have to remind you of the risk associated with such changes.*"

A murmur of unease rippled among them.

Letting them simmer in her disappointment, she resumed her stride and planted herself directly in front of us. Sandy brown hair, streaked with sun-kissed golden strands, waved to her chin. While petite, her muscular frame was pure gristle. Her uniform matched that of the others, minus the sleeves she had sliced off. Hands on her hips, the enigmatic sergeant pivoted on the ball of her foot, giving me a glimpse of the letters S.M.E.E. branded on her upper arm.

"You didn't think the ropes and bondage would be a *bit* disconcerting?" she asked her men over our heads, chin tilting in question.

"It *is* a bit off-putting." Sterling graced her with his most charming smile, which landed closer to disturbingly psychotic. "Not to mention notably uncomfortable."

Nostrils flaring, her attention snapped in his direction. "*Your* comfort is of no concern of mine."

Shrinking back, Sterling pulled his chin to his chest like a scolded child.

"We sought only to get them to you, Sergeant," a timid voice quaked. "Sh–should we untie them?"

Head falling back, she peered skyward, as if needing a moment to digest that level of stupid. "Would you like *him* to see them like this? Don't you think he would find such a spectacle *bothersome*?"

A collective gasp shuddered through the crowd.

"A thousand apologies." Footsteps scurried behind us, trembling hands cutting us loose.

The minute I was free, I attempted to shoot to my feet only to be forced back down by a meaty paw.

Hands clasped behind her back, the sergeant stared down the bridge of her nose with mild amusement. "I suggested they not tie you like animals, *not* that they let you go. Don't make me question my civility."

Rubbing the angry red skin of my wrists, I countered her glower with a hateful sneer all my own. "Phin, you doing all right?"

Out of the corner of my eye, I caught his dutiful nod while his lips continued their incessant psalm of hope.

"Good. Because we're going to walk out of here when this is over. I promise you that." Lifting my chin, I dared the sergeant to argue and crush the spirit of a child.

Lips coiling into a cynical smile, she paced before us, narrowed stare never wavering. "I am Sergeant Malyn E'toil Esquire, protector of the peace of Marooner's Rock and officer of the nobleman that stakes claim to this land. *Nothing* happens here without my knowledge, and you boys were creating quite a ruckus. *That*, I cannot allow."

"She's terrifying," Sterling uttered in an urgent whisper, his scarred jaw swinging slack. "It's breathtakingly erotic."

"Do shut up," I hissed in response.

Gnawing on the inside of her cheek, Sergeant E'toil deliberated over our presence. "It takes a brave man or an imbecile to travel to unknown realms. How would the three of you classify yourselves? Brave, or stupid?"

Sterling's head tipped in contemplation. "I would say both," he merrily chirped. "I feel it adds to my charm."

"If you think you're helping, you're not," I spat out of the corner of my mouth.

Assuming a wide-legged stance, the sergeant's stare flicked over me as if weighing my merit and finding me lacking. "Look at your puffed chest and fiery stare. You reek of a man with a mission. What great purpose was it that brought you here?"

Lifting my chin, I challenged her with silence.

"Don't feel like talking?" Smile widening with wicked delight, Malyn snapped her fingers at her men. "Bring the boy."

"Keep your hands off him!" Lunging forward, I was held back by two of her burly cronies. Another grabbed Phin by the elbow with brutish force. Dragging him to his feet, the bearded underling delivered him to his sergeant's side.

Brushing the hair from Phin's eyes, Malyn offered him the welcoming smile of a hungry crocodile. "What's your name, lad?"

"Phin, ma'am." His voice betrayed him by wavering.

"Phin, do you know what this is?" Malyn tapped the scar on her arm.

"It's a–a brand, m–ma'am," he stammered.

"Smart boy. Such a mark is made by scorching metal that burns into the skin." Her words came in an ominous hiss of malicious intent.

"We're searching for a mirror!" Sterling erupted, his eyes glassy with tears on the frightened boy's behalf. His scars proved his experience with torture to be a violently intimate one he couldn't stand back and watch an innocent child endure.

"Sterling!" I barked, before he could offer further details.

Forehead puckering, the smile vanished from Malyn's face. "A mirror? How could such a trivial item prompt a quest of this magnitude?"

"*Tell her nothing!*" I interjected, my blood audibly pulsing in my ears.

"Oh, I wouldn't advise that," Sergeant E'toil purred. Clamping a hand on Phin's shoulder, she pivoted him to face us.

"*You have never seen true torture!*" Sterling erupted. Face reddening, the tendons in his neck bulged. "For if you had, you would never request such a thing from me!"

A momentary hush fell, only to be broken by the sergeant's nudging prompt. "This mirror ..."

Casting my stare to the ground, I clamped my mouth shut.

Sterling's face sagged with defeat. "It is said to have magical properties that, when wielded properly, can answer all questions and decipher the path of destiny."

Whispers rumbled through the horde which Sergeant E'toil silenced with one raised finger. "And what plans have you for this clairvoyant receptacle if you find it?"

Lifting his face to hers, Sterling met her calculating questions with utmost honesty. "There's a dying queen that we hope to save. Then, we would very much like to go home, ma'am."

Malyn's tongue tapped against her front teeth. "Bring them, boys!" she hollered after a contemplative beat, hand swinging in a circular gesture for them to round us up. "We venture back to camp!"

Sucking in a collective gasp, the crew hesitated to move.

"Sergeant," the monstrous man who knocked me out muttered in a gentle timbre that comically contradicted his off-putting size, "are you sure *he* can handle ... outsiders?"

"*If* such a mirror is on the island, it belongs to *him*." Tone leaving no room for discussion, she released Phin and allowed the boy to dart to my side. He latched on like a drowning man on a buoy. "He alone decides what becomes of his artifacts. Factor in that he has undoubtedly detected their presence, and we will all fair *far* worse if we attempted to hide such things from him."

When they dared dawdle further still, Sergeant E'toil's lip curled from her teeth. *"Fall in line, or I'll see to it he skins every one of you alive!"*

Fumbling over each other, they rushed to gather their gear, and us. Seized by my upper arm, I was yanked to my feet. There, Malyn met me with a good-natured pat to the cheek. "Brace yourself, lad. It's time to meet the captain."

"Sh–should we take their w–weapons?" the big guy stammered.

Sergeant E'toil eyed the dagger at my hip with mild interest. "Let them keep them. If the captain doesn't take well to their company, they should at least have a fighting chance at survival."

CHAPTER FIFTEEN

Don't speak unless spoken to." Hands behind her back, Malyn glanced over her shoulder at Sterling. "Actually, not you. Try not to speak at all. The less he notices you, the better."

Tent flaps rippled on either side of us, their occupants peeking out to steal a glimpse. Before us, a ship with mahogany stain and yellow trim had run aground and sat slightly askew. Where it could have come from, I couldn't say. I had yet to see a body of water big enough for such a vessel. As far as I could tell she must've fallen from the sky.

Inching closer, Phin's little hand curled around the bottom hem of my shirt. Feeling every one of the questions scrawled on his face, I offered him a smile of comfort I knew didn't reach my eyes.

"These men greatly fear their captain," Sterling muttered in an urgent whisper, practically gnawing a hole in his lower lip. "Do we have a plan for if such a man decides to kill us?"

"I have these images skirting through my mind I can't let myself entertain," I began, the words leaving my lips in a barely audible hush, "of hulking beasts comprised of shadow. These savage aborigines stand ready and able for battle if their presence is needed. Constructed as a safeguard, they can be brought to life with a thought."

Sterling blinked my way in confusion. "Translation?"

Tipping my chin in his direction, I caught his stare and held it firm. "If the situation calls for it, I'm going to think particularly unhappy thoughts."

Treating himself to a calming breath, relief washed over his features.

Coming to a halt, Sergeant E'toil turned our way, her men assuming a half circle formation behind us. Each stood ramrod straight. Time served under their captain showing itself in the uneasy way they shifted their feet, and wiped their sweaty palms on the front of their pants.

The boards of the gangplank creaked, and each crew member sucked in a sharp intake of breath. Even the largest among them cast their stares to the ground. I thought to copy their posture. But, be it moxie or blatant stupidity, I chose instead to watch the descent of a man that instilled such fear into the hearts of many.

Thump, hiss.

Thump, hiss.

His peg leg proved the stronger of the two, forcing the other uncooperative limb onward. Still, it wasn't enough. The mammoth of a man who hit me earlier offered his captain the stability of his crooked arm, guiding the shriveled old man down toward his waiting crew. Upon closer inspection, the big guy had the innocent face of a child. An odd contrast to his ogre-like stature. Yet, it was him they feared.

Posture curled in, the captain's free arm was tucked tight to his chest. A scraggly grey beard swung to his midsection, the length fastened in two distinct knots. Time had sunk his face into harsh lines and a sallow complexion, shriveling his form to bone.

Dragging his tongue over his top teeth, Sterling's lips parted with a *pop*. "I was expecting someone … meatier," he mused, only to be shushed by the men within earshot.

Feet scuffing in the dirt, the captain paused at the base of the gangplank to let his sleepy gaze sweep over the crowd. At the sight of our trio, he winced. Bloodshot eyes bulged with interest.

Tipping toward his mountainous aide, he rasped in death's weak rattle, "Potchis, did you ring the chimes?"

"Thrice, Captain. Same as always." The man I now knew as Potchis tied his stare to the ground and refused to let it stray.

The captain's jaw worked, chewing on his face as he deliberated. "Thrice more, if you please. It soothes me."

Unweaving himself from the Captain's hold, Potchis presented a cane for him to lean upon, patiently waiting until he was steady before stepping away. Edging back, the towering man-child stirred a wind chime comprised of glass jars and silverware. Music as soft as fairy bells tinkled through the camp. The rest of the crew stiffened at the sound, a few emitting muted whimpers.

When the chimes stilled, Potchis returned to his captain's side and guided him the remaining distance to us. Scuffing through the dirt, the pair moved at a pace a snail would find tiresome. They arrived in a waft of sour breath and body odor.

The captain's cloudy grey stare shifted from Sterling, to me, to Phin, and back again. The index finger of his crippled hand twitched incessantly.

Jaw working, he snorted Sterling's way. "Your mouth is odd."

"Your face is old," Sterling shot back, his tone not one of malice but fact.

As a chorus of gasps rocked his crew, the captain merely nodded in agreement. "So true." Point of his hooked nose jerking in my direction, he tossed his question to Malyn. "This be he? The soul who brought all the changes to our land?"

"One and the same." Flanking her decrepit leader, the chilling dagger of her emotionless stare sliced into me. "Mermaids, birds, butterflies, and flowers the likes of which I have never seen. Our world has changed, my captain. Yet nothing is irreversible. One shudder that it bothers you, and it will *all* be erased from Marooner's Rock by any means necessary."

"Easy, child." The captain's attempt at a chuckle morphed into a hacking cough. Eyes watering, he wheezed down a few labored breaths before regaining the ability to speak. "Ensure a crime has been committed before you string a man up."

"Yes, Captain," she muttered, heels clicking together with her formal salute.

Tipping his frail head my way, he offered me a compassionate half-smile. "Apologies, friend. Sergeant E'toil tends to be of a harsh, military mind. My name is Captain James Harwood, and who might you be?"

Chest puffed in the regal stature insisted upon by my commanding officers, I squared my shoulders and spoke with due respect to Captain Harwood. "My name is Alastor, member of Atlantica's Royal Guard under reigning King Triton—although I assume he suspects me dead by now."

"Atlantica?" he croaked, spittle bubbling on his pale and cracked lips. "The underwater kingdom?"

"One and the same." My head dipped in a nod of confirmation.

"In that case, you've ventured to the wrong realm. Not an ocean to be found! A dire situation for mer and pirates alike." Harwood's cackle disintegrated into yet another coughing fit.

Potchis shook a handkerchief from his pocket and offered it to his captain who used it to dab at his foam-covered lips.

"I can only hope to fare half as well as you have here," came my polite rebuttal.

Seemingly finished with me, Captain Harwood shuffled on, his lips grinding over his gums. Waddling a few shuffled steps farther, he paused in front of a pallid Phin. The frightened boy swallowed hard, his grip tightening on the wood flute clutched in his hands.

Hunching his back, Harwood stooped as far as he could to come eye level with Phin. "What say you, lad? What do *you* think of Marooner's Rock?"

Phin glanced my way, chin quivering in need for reassurance.

A blink and a smile were the only encouragement I could offer.

"I-I liked the mermaid lagoon." The lad's voice cracked. "Th-the creatures there were quite enchanting."

Snorting in contempt, Malyn rolled her shoulders and clasped her hands behind her back. "Frivolous enchantment does not assure the safety and serenity of our people. We aren't allowed the poetry of such musings."

"Oh, do lighten up, E'toil." Captain Harwood rolled his eyes with mock exasperation, a simple gesture that earned a titter of laughter from the anxious boy.

Malyn's expression softened a degree, giving her the appearance of a teenager annoyed by her zany grandfather's antics. "I thought it was my intricate attention to detail and insistence on good form which secured my title among this horde of miscreants?"

"And, so it is." Folding the handkerchief over his arthritic fingers, the captain handed it back to Potchis. "Still I feel you've overreacted this time. You feared I would be so bothered by these newcomers, yet here I am. My same ole crotchety self." Casting a glance to Phin, he gave the boy a wink.

"I am thrilled to admit this was my mistake, Captain." Sergeant E'toil twirled her index finger in a circular formation, signaling for the crew to return to their normal activities.

As they scurried off, Harwood reached down with one quaking hand and pretended to steal Phin's nose.

I'd like to think what happened next was circumstance. That my thoughts *didn't* get the better of me, conjuring forth a silvery butterfly simply to see what would happen.

Be that as it may, I saw it in my mind mere seconds before the shimmering specimen fluttered into the camp.

Grown men clasped hands at the sight of it, chins dropping to their chests as they muttered prayers for mercy.

Leaning heavily on his cane, Harwood stilled to watch it flap by.

Sterling's head spun in one direction, then the other, lips sinking into a frown. "Without knowing the cast of characters, I'm having trouble staying interested in this farce."

"*Quiet, man!*" I hissed, the palpable tension setting my nerves on edge.

Malyn wasted no time. Skirting along the edge of the clearing, she scooped up a burlap sack and held it at her side in a white-knuckled fist.

The air seemed to be sucked from the space, all eyes focused on the rickety old man.

"My mother used to love butterflies so." Harwood forced one trembling hand up to shoulder height. Instead of flapping off, the lovely creature landed on the first knuckle of his forefinger. Easing his arm down, he peered tenderly at his passenger. "When she worked in the garden, they would hover around her in the most divine halo. A few would come to rest in her golden hair. Far more exquisite accessories than any man-made comb or barrette."

With each second that passed, the crew grew more anxious. Nervous stares drifted to the path behind them. These men wanted to run, were clamping their lips down on brewing screams. But why?

Once more, it seemed fate answered a question I hadn't the nerve to voice. A blink and Harwood's eyes rolled back to reptilian slits. His voice dropped to a demonic hiss. "Even when I found her slumped over the petunias, they were floating around her like merry little fairies of death."

Sprinting to shield us, Malyn threw her arms out wide. "Get the boy back!"

Her gruff warning, demanding flight or fight, prompted me to curl my hand around the fabric of Phin's collar and shuffle him behind me. Whatever was coming, whatever beastly fate threatened to consume us, would have to go through me first.

"Sterling, back up," I hissed, stare darting from him to the captain and back again. "Right now. Get out of the way."

His head turned slowly in my direction, pupils constricted to panicked points. "Snake in the hen house," he whispered. Fear rooted him in that spot, his legs visibly shaking.

As a chorus of sickening pops and gruesome squishes elicited screams from the crew, I seized Sterling's wrist and threw him behind Phin and I. Positioning myself protectively before them, I swiveled in the captain's direction. The impossibility of what I saw, swung my jaw slack.

Starting at the crown of his skull, Harwood's skin peeled away in a series of ghastly slurps and gurgles. Cracking bone allowed his slight stature to swell to a behemoth frame. Chunks of human flesh fell to the ground with wet slaps, revealing a thick, reptilian hide beneath.

Phin shielded his eyes behind me as the nightmare of teeth and scales emerged. The stench of the transformation held tidings of home, a fishy stench wafting on the breeze. Transformation complete, the captain rose on two legs before us, appearing more crocodile than human. Jaw protruding in a harsh underbite, rows of jagged teeth sawed his face into a deadly smile. Glowing amber eyes glared my way, as his viciously hooked talons clicked together in eager anticipation.

A low rumble emanated from the crocodile, his head slowly swiveling in Sterling's direction. *"You've suffered, brother. I know such struggles well."*

Whirling around, Sterling folded Phin against his chest, squeezing his own eyes shut tight. "Don't look, child. Everything will be all right. Just … look away."

"It wasn't a threat," I muttered, numb with shock.

Other than their brazen sergeant, not one among the crew dared to move or breathe, each opting to play opossum lest they be chosen as an evening snack.

Focused on results, Malyn extended her free hand, creeping closer to the beast on silent steps. "Captain? I know you're still in there. Can you hear me?"

An unholy chuckle reverberated from the croc-man, his lips curling into a snarl. *"Shouting at the wind would be as useful as calling to your captain. He has abandoned you all."*

The demonic chill of his voice sliced me to the bone, each word reverberating through me.

"Captain," Malyn attempted again, "if you are there, I need you to stand down!"

"He answered," I managed in a weak and raspy croak.

"Do not move on me, girl." Flipping his head, croc-man snapped his jaw in ravenous threat. *"I will shred the flesh from your bones. You know not the evil you serve."*

"Captain James Harwood!" she persisted, tendons bulging. *"Stand down!* This is your final warning."

"Stop." Forgetting how to blink, I reached out for her. As if such a paltry gesture could hold back the tide of war. "Can't you hear him?"

Pointed tongue dragging over his teeth, the croc's slitted glare darted my way. *"Save your counsel, lad. She neither knows nor cares that she's the handmaiden to the devil."*

Blood screaming in my ears, I watched life slow to a crawl. "They can't ... hear."

Battle cry tearing from her lungs, Malyn threw the burlap sack aside to reveal her weapon. No sword gleamed from her grasp, but a ticking clock she hoisted high for all to see. Cued by the act, her men found their feet and stumbled for their own hidden stashes. Behind their backs. Tucked beneath trees. Hidden in tents. Awkwardly stuffed down their trousers. Clock after clock appeared. Each brandished high and proud in a union I couldn't begin to comprehend.

Complexion paling from deep emerald to a mossy hue, the croc-man hissed at the sight of them. Saliva dripped from his exposed fangs.

"The hands of time tick, monster!" Malyn stalked forward, each step stabbing her intent into his leathery hide. "Every second counts down the time you have left."

Skirting around the perimeter, her men surrounded the croc, inching closer in a tightening circle.

Guarded attention sweeping over the horde stalking him, the glow of his reptilian gaze locked on me. Pulling back, he charged.

Grabbing handfuls of Sterling's shirt, I shoved him and Phin as far away as possible before one clawed hand closed around my throat. Croc-man yanked my feet from the ground, drawing me close enough to see the bits of meat and flesh stuck between his incisors, his rank breath assaulting my senses.

The crew swarmed around us. Their clocks swung inches from our faces, ticking and tocking in a pounding chorus that drummed out rational thought.

"*Take the boy and run.*" Weakening by the moment, the croc's complexion dulled to a waxen grey. While his stare bore into me, he depleted the last of his energy ensuring his message was received. "*Elsewise ... no one leaves this never-land.*"

He eased me to the ground gentle as he could before crumbling to his knees in the dirt. Locked in the silence of my own ineptitude, I could do nothing but watch as the droning of the clocks peeled back the reptilian façade in the same grisly manner by which it appeared.

Captain Harwood, drenched with sweat and gasping for air, fell in a heap beside me. He had not, however, come out of the transformation unmarred. Claws protruded from the fingers of his left hand. A smattering of scales poked out from beneath the shredded cloth of what had once been his shirt.

A mask of confusion cutting deep lines between his brows, the captain spoke the exact sentiment rattling through my jumbled mind. "Wh–what happened?"

CHAPTER SIXTEEN

The wood flute's tune flooded the space, its melancholy notes reflecting the mood of their troubled musician. At the orders of Sergeant E'toil, we had been assigned a shanty at the edge of camp. It was little more than four walls and tin roof, with a small hearth on the far wall to ward off the night's chill. Orange sparks sprayed from the fire within as I stoked it.

Setting the poker aside, I pivoted in my squat and dropped one knee to the ground. Eye level with the pensive boy, I ducked my head in attempt to catch his stare. "Phin? Are you well? We can talk about what transpired out there, if you like."

Shaking his head, he played on.

Dragging my tongue over my chapped lower lip, I tried again. "I found what happened unsettling. That doesn't make me weak, merely human ... of sorts."

A haunting reprieve via that flute was his only response.

"You remember I can make things happen here, don't you?" Shifting on to both knees, I sank back on my heels. "In my mind I see the shadows around this dusty hut becoming our soldiers. Massive, heaving warriors that would keep us safe if the crocodile were to come back. Would it grant you a bit of peace if I made them real?"

Finally, Phin pulled the flute from his lips, and rested it carefully in his lap. When his gaze dragged up to mine, it was not one of traumatized angst, as I expected, but a quiet stillness. "I appreciate your concern, sir. Truly, I do. Yet in that moment, when the beast appeared, I felt no fear. Do you know why?"

My head tilted with interest. "I couldn't begin to fathom. At your age such a thing would have had me shrieking until my gills collapsed."

While the hint of a smile toyed at the corners of Phin's thin lips, a cloud of sadness blew in to darken his eyes. "When my mother was alive and in good health, she used to tuck me in with a story every night. Perched beside me on the bed, she would stroke my hair, and tell tales of gods and goddesses with unimaginable powers. My favorite was the god Pan, who ruled over nature and the wild. The forest and its residents, both big and small, eagerly bent to his command."

"Sounds like a fun bloke, to be sure."

Resting his elbows on his knees, Phin leaned in. His voice dropped to a secretive whisper. "I wasn't scared of the monster, because *Pan* was there ... with me. I walked with him through this land, watching nature respond to his every whim. It was he that threw me to safety in the face of harm, assuring me there is nothing here for me to fear."

"*Me?*" I squawked, pulling back in shock. "You think *me* to be Pan?"

Phin's brows lifted to his hairline, daring me to argue. "Do you have another answer for being capable of such marvels? Whom, except Pan, could accomplish what you have?"

I contemplated protesting, but saw little point in stealing that which brought the lad comfort. "Phin," I relented, "I have no other explanations to give."

His face brightened with the glow of a thousand candles. "I knew it," he gasped. "While I appreciate your offer of the shadow army, I have no need for it with you here. However, you may want to float the idea past ... *him*." His gaze drifted skyward.

A soft rap at the door gifted me a momentary pardon from that peculiar conversation. Rising to my feet, I shook out my cramping legs. "We will give him another minute or two, and hope he comes down on his own." Ruffling Phin's hair, I skirted around him and strode to the door.

"Man to croc. Croc to man. How can the flesh be both?" a hushed voice pondered from above.

"Hang in there, mate!" I tossed the encouragement in passing, and yanked open the door, only to bristle at our visitor. "Sergeant E'toil."

Straightening her hunched shoulders, Malyn shifted from one foot to the other. "I–I brought fresh water from the well." Lifting the pitcher cradled in her hands, her soldier façade cracked with concern. "I thought the boy may need some. Is he okay?"

Crossing my arms over my chest, I leaned against the door frame. "I would invite you in to evaluate his condition, but feel we first need to discuss if you can transform into any type of reptile or other assorted creature? It's a question I would have never thought to ask before, yet here it seems a crucial conversation topic."

"The captain is the only one amongst us that is cursed in such a fashion," she said, daring a step closer. "I give you my word on that."

Silently, I stepped back and allowed her access. Brushing past me, she smelled of sunshine and pine needles.

"Thank you. I really feel quite—" Head falling back, Malyn stared up at the ceiling. "Are you aware your friend is in the rafters?"

"He's processing things. He'll come down when he's ready."

"Am I allowed to know he wears two skins? Does knowing too much make me mad? I didn't want to know! Take it back! Retract that wriggling larva of information from my brain before it hatches!" Sterling's panicked hiss wafted down.

"He may be a while," I deadpanned.

Setting the pitcher down on the rickety table, Malyn wiped her sweaty palms on the front of her trousers and edged in the direction of Phin. The soft serenade of his flute drew her in, softening her harsh soldier's stride to a careful tiptoe. Dropping to her knees, she folded her hands in her lap and patiently waited for his concert to conclude.

Lost in the music, Phin let the notes carry him far beyond the shanty walls. Lashes brushing the tops of his cheeks, he played a capricious little tune that conjured images of grand adventures, and a life of endless whimsy. Tune tinkling to a close, Phin retracted his instrument and wet his parched lips. Only then did he acknowledge the sergeant with a soft smile.

"Did you like the song?" he asked in place of a greeting, chestnut locks falling across his forehead.

"I loved it," she gushed, the sentiment slathered with sincerity. "It has been a long while since I have heard music of any kind, other than the wind chimes. I forgot how much I missed a sweet melody."

Sheepishly, he cast his stare to the flute and dragged his thumb lovingly over the carved edge of it. "Deep in the refrain, that's where I find home."

Such a downtrodden sentiment uttered by one so young seemed to remind the sergeant why she was there. Spine straightening, she swallowed hard before approaching the tender topic. "I suppose one would want to escape after the spectacle you witnessed tonight."

Phin's head rose, wisdom well beyond his years sharpening his stare. "You care for the crocodile, not just the man."

Head listing, she pressed, "What makes you say that?"

"There have to be far more effective ways to drive back such a beast," he pointed out, index finger tracing over his initials in the flute. "Yet you found a method humane and gentle. By my eyes, that seems an act of compassionate mercy."

Lips pressed in a thin line, Malyn nodded. "How very astute of you. And true at that. I do. Enough to protect him from himself."

"You're … friends?" he questioned with growing interest. Shifting in his seat, the chair creaked under his slight weight.

Malyn flopped down on her rump and crossed her legs beneath her, a small cloud of dust kicking up from the rotting floorboards. "He's more like … my protector."

Sterling's face swung down between them, dangling upside down as he adjusted his positioning in the beams. "I, for one, would love to hear that tale."

Shooting him a sideways glance of annoyance, she honored the request. "It's not an original story for life's woes to begin with one's parentage, yet I count myself among that lot. Seldom in my travels have I encountered a man as harsh and stern as my own father. A lifelong soldier to the crown, he worked his way up the ranks and vested his entire self-worth on the lofty title he earned. He and his first wife had a son they named James, my brother who I would never meet. He was raised to follow father's footsteps, and did so with vigor. Joining the king's fleet the very day he was of age, he earned a spot on the front lines at the Battle of Briar. He never made it home." Catching a string at the bottom hem of her pant leg, she twirled it around her finger before ripping it off. "I don't know what disappointed father more; the loss of his only child, or the insult of knowing James had allowed himself to be killed in battle. Knowing Father, it was the latter. From that moment on, Father became obsessed with producing an heir to pick up the yoke poor James dropped. Both he and his wife being advanced in years, such a goal became a biologically lofty one. Father refused to let such a hinderance slow or stop him. Through his connection in the castle, he learned of a young maiden—well-bred, with a hefty dowry— whose father had recently succumbed to the fevers. She and her mother needed the protection of a strong pairing to hold their place in court. That was all the motivation Father needed. He divorced his first wife under the claim she could not produce a second heir for him and married my mother, Violet."

"How noble of him," I snorted, scratching a hand over the back of my neck.

"Not in the least," she countered, one brow lifted in open contempt. "My mother was the purest, most gentle soul you could ever hope to meet. A cross word thrown at her was the equivalent to kicking a puppy. Even so, he threw vile sentiments at her incessantly after she had the audacity to give birth to a *female* child … namely, me. When the years passed, and his boy failed to appear, Father concluded that there was no reason why *I* couldn't become the soldier he so desired. From that point on, I was no longer allowed to play with dolls, wear lovely dresses, or even talk with other girls. I had to fight. Had to train. So many lessons to learn carrying buckets of water in the pouring rain, while being verbally berated. My hair was sheared short—a habit I have yet to let go of. When my womanly bosom began to bud, I was wrapped tight to the point of pain. All the while, I looked on longingly while other girls studied poetry, curled their hair, and twirled in pretty gowns. Never again would such silken fabrics grace my skin."

Cramming my hands into the pockets of my slacks, I shook my head. "I lost my father before I ever knew him. Your tale reminds me there are far worse things."

"Different degrees of the same sorrow, I'd imagine," Malyn muttered. Staring into the fire, she took us with her into her reverie. "Father enlisted me to service of the crown when I came of age. My military career began with simply trying to find a place to station me. Women weren't allowed to fight on the battlefield. Guarding the king was a position that had to be earned. Where, then, could they plant a young girl that felt only with a chest full of medals could she ever earn her father's acceptance?"

Not one among us dared to guess the verdict of such a sensitive conundrum.

"They placed me on the royal fleet." Hands running up and down her arms, Malyn fought off a chill only she felt. "Hardly the right place for a girl, since sailors considered a female on board to be bad luck. Still, the commanding officers insisted that I would be safe there. Silly, stupid men. They believed their command to be iron clad and ensured my protection. Such rules don't apply in the middle of the vast ocean." Tears welling in her eyes, she blinked hard to chase them away. "I thank my father for raising me to be ruthless. I can say with heartfelt honestly that if it wasn't for his ceaseless training I never would have made it off that ship. The vessel's seaward name was *The Enforcer*. I see that now as the foreboding warning it was. As if it was predicting what I had to become to protect not just my virtue, but my life. I was challenged and assaulted, time and time again. All hours of the day and night. No mercy granted for physical exhaustion, I spent every moment fighting off any and all advances with a brutality I shouldn't be proud of, but—gods help me—I truly am. Fixating on one truth got me through each day: fight, win, *live*. And live I did. Exhausted, beaten down, afraid to so much as close my eyes ... yet *alive*. For how much longer I could have kept on, I can't say. Eventually, one would have bested me. Of that I have no doubt. I was their obsession, and they wouldn't stop until one beat me."

Trailing off, she plunged into silence at the horrors she faced and the repulsive acts she narrowly escaped.

I swallowed hard. I was almost afraid to ask, but had to know. "How did you secure freedom?"

"I was swabbing the deck, lip still bleeding from my last brawl, when I saw the black sails of the Jolly Roger cresting the horizon." Peering out the opened door at the same landbound vessel, a sense of peace washed over her, softening her ache like a mother's soothing touch. "Not that I knew it as that at the time. I have looked back on that moment over the years, trying to recall how it felt when I gazed up at my salvation for the first time. As much as I can recall, I don't remember feeling anything at all. I saw it as another hurdle to jump just to make it to another sunset. While I watched it swell before us, the rest of the crew scurried about, shouting orders at one another. Pirates had been spotted, and that brotherhood of so-called upstanding sailors sought nothing more than to sink them to the depths." A dry huff of laughter escaping her, Malyn's stare locked on the Jolly Roger askew in the distance, seeing it for the first time once more. "As if they stood a chance. Time moved in a dizzying blur. Our ship was overtaken, the pirates boarded it and trapped the crew in a trembling huddle on the main deck. I can still hear the echoing clomps of Captain Harwood's boots against the plank strung between the two vessels. That was before he lost his leg to cannon fire, you see. Back then his presence was undeniable. He possessed a command over the sea and all those that dared charter a vessel upon it. At the sight of him, the same men who tormented me without mercy now sobbed and wept for their mommies. I later learned that *The Enforcer* and its gutless captain were in possession of an artifact Harwood desired. What it was, I never asked. I didn't care to know what they deemed the value of my worth."

"Your worth?" Phin scoot closer beside Malyn, staring up at the unshed tears gleaming in her eyes with youthful concern.

For his sake, she attempted a smile that fell short of reaching her eyes. "The crew propositioned the captain to take me, in exchange for their safe passage."

"The captain took you?" Phin's hands twisted around his flute, clutching it to his chest. "That doesn't make him sound much like a hero."

"In that regard it doesn't, does it?" Head listing, she brushed the hair from Phin's eyes. "Captain Harwood seemed to consider the idea. Testing their resolve, he asked if they would give any protest to me becoming entertainment for the crew. They voiced no objections. Feeding off the weakness of their character, he asked if they would like to watch as his men shredded me to ribbons. The lot of them looked away, too ashamed to meet his eyes. The final degradation was to inquire if they would voice a complaint to me being hung from the mast and quartered, bathing them all in my blood and entrails. A few whimpers were the only protest offered. Evaluation of their valor complete, Captain ordered his men to claim the ship's booty then sink her to the depths. When he turned my way, I convulsed with terror, so sure was I that my death sentence was about to be uttered. To my surprise—and the crew's horror—he said that since they were willing to decide my fate, it was only fair I be allowed to reciprocate. Voice devoid of emotion, he asked who among them I chose to spare."

"What did you do?" Needing a moment to find my voice, the words came out in a breathless whisper.

Pushing off the floor, Malyn walked to the fire and lost herself in its crackling embers. "I looked out over their sea of faces, searching for a morsel of good among them. There was Samuel, who snuck me an extra biscuit each night. Then went on to crack my rib when his friends goaded him into challenging me. Seemingly compassionate Martin said he would guard the door to the infirmary, and allow me to sleep. He later crept in during the wee hours of morning to try and take liberties with my battered body. Should I have shown mercy to William, who actually came to my defense once and said I owed him something for it later? In the end, I uttered one word. *None*," she confessed to the flames. "There were no survivors. That was the first time I watched the crocodile appear. He ravaged *The Enforcer* and left none standing. Their shrieks still haunt my nightmares. When the last body fell, he stalked back onto the Jolly Roger with gore tripping from his fangs. Pausing beside me, his panted breath reeked of death. He could have killed me like all the others. I still question why he didn't. Instead, he loomed beside me, wordlessly watching the ocean swallow the once proud *Enforcer*." Slowly turning our way, Malyn rubbed her hands up and down her upper arms, fighting off the chill of her sordid revelation. "I've been a grateful member of his crew ever since. You should know, the transformation wreaks havoc on his body. He has aged decades in the five years I've served under him. I do all I can to prevent his change; seeking to control and maintain all elements of Marooner's Rock. Ours is an island of nothing. Even the weather is a testimony of neutrality. All of that changed when the three of you appeared. Whatever business you have here is of no concern of mine. My sole focus is to keep the monster at bay, and my captain safe."

"Monster. What does such a word mean?" Dropping from the ceiling, Sterling melted from the rafters. Mid-fall, he flipped in the air and landed gracefully on his feet. "If one is deemed a monster, isn't any act they commit considered a monstrous one? Simply by being, they are a monster behaving monstrously. As a loon acts looney, or a duck acts … ducky. It is their very nature. Who they are. Not wrong. Not right. Not good, nor bad. Connotations to the contrary are based purely on critical judgments."

"Someone interject *something*," I requested, lips falling into a mock frown, "because that actually made sense to me, and that's terrifying."

Bristling, my quip bounced off Malyn's indignant front. She swiveled to face Sterling, her hands balled into tight fists at her sides. "What is it you're implying, sir?"

"I imply nothing." He shrugged. "You call the thing within him a monster. As it is a faction of your captain, that would make your captain a monster as well. By definition then, every act he commits would be considered monstrous. It seems to me he would be a tough fellow to trust."

Malyn stalked a circle around him, glaring him down with predatory intent. "We all have some sort of monster within us. Greed. Longing. Rage. Do you deny the daily fight we all endure not to give in to the dark voice whispering in our minds, tempting us to lose ourselves in unthinkable atrocities?"

"I would never," Sterling simply stated, unruffled by her aggression.

She planted her feet in a wide-legged stance and jammed her hands onto her hips. "While the captain's darkness manifests for all to see, it doesn't make the beast in each of us any less real."

Raising his hand in front of him, Sterling watched with mesmerized interest as his fingers rolled and twisted one way and then the other. "Well and true. How can we trust anyone … or, ourselves?"

Malyn filled her lungs to capacity, and exhaled through pursed lips in effort to maintain her slipping composure. "I trust the captain, because without him I would be dead." Marching to the door, she threw a glance back over her shoulder. "Perhaps you'll think him less the dastardly villain when you learn he has granted you access to the mirror."

Hands on his knees, Sterling crouched down beside Phin to whisper, "Did I call him such a thing? I don't remember using those words at all. Then again, I seldom listen to my own yammerings."

A threatening laugh pinkened Phin's cheeks, pulling at the corners of his lips. Wisely, he suppressed it.

Hand on the door frame, Malyn drummed her fingers against the weathered wood. "The captain is resting now. The change exhausts him. When he rises, you shall go before him to investigate the artifact under supervision."

"And *after* we have viewed the mirror?" I ventured.

Tipping her chin, she peered my way with an icy indifference that prickled through me. "After, Captain Harwood will determine if you live or die."

CHAPTER SEVENTEEN

The fire had died down. Moonlight glistened through the glassless windows, bathing the shanty in a silver glow. Silently staring at the smoldering embers within the hearth, our trio perked at the crunch of heavy footfalls approaching. Glancing to the door, we found Potchis swaying there. Cradled in his hands, he toted what appeared to be a homemade teddy bear comprised of mismatched fabrics and loosely strung button-eyes.

"For the boy." He extended the offering in Phin's direction. "A lad needs something to hold onto, especially when there's no one to hold *him*."

Phin's eyes, heavy with sleep, brightened at the sight of the toy. Dragging himself to his feet, he scuffed across the creaking floorboards to collect it. "Thank you," he murmured, squeezing it tight to his chest.

A curt nod was as close to a response as Potchis offered. Frame filling the doorway, the giant I was coming to see as the gentle sort shifted his weight from one foot to the other. "All must come. The captain awaits."

Hopping to his feet, Sterling shook off sleep's hold with an aggressive shudder. "I do hope he lets us keep our heads. I've grown rather attached to mine."

Oblivious to how he frightened the child, causing Phin to clutch his toy tighter still, Sterling strode out the door without glancing back to see if the rest of us were following.

Having to step into the shanty to allow Sterling passage, Potchis ducked his head to catch Phin's apprehensive stare. "Stay by me. I'll keep you safe."

Phin reached out and closed his fist around two of Potchis' fingers, trusting the towering chap to lead him out.

Trailing the odd pair, I was struck by the lengths Potchis was going to for the safety and security of a child he barely knew.

"Potchis," I ventured, a gentle night breeze causing rogue strands of hair to lash at my cheeks, "are you happy here, serving your captain?"

Head bobbing, his hunched stature didn't break stride. "Potchis is part of the crew, he is."

"That's not much of an answer," Phin pointed out, the lilt of his voice an angel's song compared to Potchis' thunderous boom.

For a moment Potchis let his gaze travel to the tree line at the edge of camp, something that resembled longing cut deep creases between his brows. "Potchis leaving was never a question. Being part of the crew … was."

Maybe I saw in him the part of myself that longed for freedom, and home. Maybe I was a dog with a bone that didn't know when to let go. Unsure of my own motivation, I dug in further. "But if it was? What if you were given the choice to leave a free man, or stay? What would you choose?"

Steps faltering, Potchis' head whipped in one direction then the other, scanning the landscape as if worried someone was listening. "Part of the crew," he stated again, with a stern conviction that rang false.

Solidifying from the darkness in a chilling shimmer, Sterling offered Potchis a wide, manic smile. His eyes glowing orbs that haunted the night. "Every adventure requires a first step. You simply must choose which is yours."

Potchis pulled back, yanking Phin along with him in panicked retreat.

Lunging forward, I clapped a comforting hand on Potchis' tree trunk of a forearm. "He means no harm!" I soothed. Desperate to calm the spiraling situation, I beseeched the lonely child that lived in the depths of the giant's stare. "He's been alone, and dejected. Same as you."

"I have?" Sterling's nose crinkled. "What a miserable existence."

"My point," hushing Sterling with a glare, I turned a friendly smile in Potchis' direction, "is that while our crew isn't much, you're welcome to join us."

"Look out for the boy? Keep him safe?" The possibility twinkling in his irises was quickly snuffed out with a glance in the direction of the Jolly Roger and its waiting captain. Shoulders sagging, Potchis' broad face folded into a frown. White wisps of hair falling into his eyes, he shook his head. "Part of the crew, he is. Never leaving this never-land."

"Of course, I meant no disrespect."

If he heard me at all, Potchis hid it well. Stillness washed over him, leaving nothing behind short of an empty shell of acceptance. Peering my way with eyes as vacant as the teddy bear's buttons, he dutifully returned to the task he had been charged with. "Can't keep the captain waiting."

Potchis pivoted on his heel, resuming his wide stride, rushing us toward our rendezvous with destiny.

Seated in a wingback chair, Captain Harwood was propped up by pillows, appearing more shriveled and frail then before. Dressed in a crimson velvet robe, he outstretched one arthritic hand to wave us into his private dining room aboard the Jolly Roger. Potchis and Malyn took their place against the wall opposite him, stares trained straight ahead as they awaited their captain's command. Entering the room, with Sterling and Phin tucked close to my sides, I scanned the space. Even in its dilapidated condition, the stately magnificence of the ship could not be denied. The mahogany table was hand-carved mastery, the walls draped with jewel toned tapestries.

"Come, join me for a meal," he rasped, his quaking hand gesturing to the chairs opposite him. "I am sorry to say I only offer what the island grants us, but you're very welcome to it."

The spread before us was barely enough to feed one person; a halved pineapple, one smoked fish, a bowl of some sort of grey mush, and another of macadamia nuts. While Sterling and Phin took their seats, I remained standing, hands gripping the back of my chair.

"May I?" I asked with a nod to the humble buffet.

The corners of his pale grey eyes crinkling with interest, Harwood bowed his head in approval of the unspoken request. "By all means."

Head falling back, I rolled my shoulders and tried to recall how it was I manifested things before. Far as I could tell, I simply thought of them. In my mind I pictured the great feast served at Caselotti. The salty sweetness of a glazed ham. Succulent roast goose. Bowls of fluffy mashed potatoes. Towering plates of warm biscuits. Fruit by the bushel. Trays of desserts I could never name, but would never forget their heavenly decadence. The vision was so vivid I could smell the mouthwatering aroma.

A bark of laughter rattling from Harwood's chest popped my eyes open.

"That is a handy skill to have!" The captain peered my way with a fresh appreciation. "I'm inclined to offer you a position with my crew with talent like that."

My chair squeaked across the wood planked floor as I dragged it back to take a seat. "Were I not duty bound to King Liam of Caselotti, I might be inclined to consider such an offer," I politely lied.

"And a man of honor, to boot. I can respect that." Scooting himself up in his seat, he waved the three of us to the now grand display. "Please, help yourselves. I would hate to enjoy all of this alone."

Phin needed no further invitation. Grabbing the polished silver spoon, he heaped his plate with mashed potatoes. Content with the helping of fluffy spoils, he dove in and enjoyed each mouthful with audible appreciation.

Watching Harwood's hand shake as it struggled to grip a serving fork, Malyn took a tentative step forward, hovering in case she was needed. Only when he managed to finagle a piece of ham onto his plate did she step back into formation.

After cutting his meat with the side of his fork, Harwood shoveled a bite into his mouth and talked in between noisy chomps.

"Many have sought answers held within the mirror you seek. Myself included. Yet, a scarce few are granted them. Sadly, I'm counted among that unfortunate lot as well. I have no qualms allowing you to gaze upon it, but would hate for you to be disappointed as I have been so many, many times."

Hungrily wetting his lips, Sterling reached over his plate to tear a drumstick from the roasted goose. The moment his skin touched it, the headless foul leapt from the tray. It flapped its featherless wings, and flew right out the open window. Hand flitting to his mouth, Sterling emitted a stunned *eep*.

With a grimace of unease, he pushed his plate in my direction. "Would you get me a slice of ham … please?"

Blinking in astonishment, the party as a collective unit decided to shake off the oddity witnessed.

"We know of the legend." I cleared my throat, and forked two slices of ham on to Sterling's plate for him. "They say it takes one pure of heart and gifted with sight to behold the truth within the reflection. If I may ask how you came to possess such a treasured artifact?"

"I sought it out for many years, hoping it would hold the key to breaking my own … curse." Reaching for his napkin to dab his mouth, his opposite hand pointed to his face in reference to his reptilian alter ego. "Tracking and researching led me to a ship known as The Enforcer. Our own Sergeant Malyn was among the treasures I found aboard."

Bristling at her name in mention to part of her own tale she had never heard, Malyn risked a glance in her captain's direction.

Fork suspended over his potatoes, Harwood leaned one elbow on the table. "I heard rumor of what was needed to access the mirror's well of truth. Knowing what it required, I chose to spare her. Wouldn't it have been poetic if that slight lass fighting for her life was the key to all knowledge? Sadly, poetry is not the way of magic. At least not in this case."

Whatever Sergeant E'toil felt at this revelation, she managed to keep her face blank of emotion. Only a series of rapid blinks clued she heard anything at all.

Beside me, Sterling slapped at a biscuit, fearing it would come alive.

"Stop it," I muttered out of the corner of my mouth.

Utensils scraping over his plate, Hardwood topped a slice of ham with a dollop of potato and popped it in his mouth. "Since then, I have taken in several wayward youths during my travels—such as Potchis there—and brought them here under the pretenses of joining my crew. Each I gave an attempt to glance in the mirror, without ever telling them the real reason why. Saw no purpose in that, they had a home here either way. After all, even a currently landbound ship needs tending to. A captain is nothing without his crew."

Unlike his sergeant, a shadow of hurt drifted over Potchis' features before the demands of his duties could chase it away.

"If I'm to tell the truth of it," picking up his stein of ale, Harwood treated himself to a hardy swallow, "I fear my time is growing short. The change is taking a harder toll now than ever before, my body failing to recover as it once did. My prayer is that the winds of fate blew you here for a reason. Mayhap we could have the boy peer into the mirror? See what he can see?" Stein returned to the table in a slosh of auburn liquid, the captain snapped his gnarled fingers at Potchis. "Lad, bring the mirror over. I don't have the strong back I once did to retrieve much of anything of weight."

Venturing to the far side of the room, wood floor creaking beneath his feet, Potchis tossed aside the black velvet shroud. Beneath was an oblong frame etched with gold scrolls and leaves. Hoisting it off its pedestal, he swung it around, giving me a momentary glimpse at its surface. The images I saw reflected were of those in the room with me, yet somehow … not. Sterling's eyes were glowing feline slits, faint stripes of blue wisped over his cheeks. Harwood's croc reflection I had to check against the real thing, fearing the beast had made a sneaky return. Disturbed as I was by both of these glimpses, they in no way prepared me for Phin's likeness. His sunken eyes were lined with dark shadows. Skin, the grey pallor of death, cracked and oozed with rot and decay. Lifeless eyes stared back at me, beseeching me to save him.

Then it was gone. The mirror turned at an angle I could no longer see into, much to my soul's relief. Propping it up on the table beside Captain Harwood, Potchis dutifully held it in place.

"Well done." Harwood barely looked up from his plate, dragging his last bite of ham through the remnants of his potatoes.

To my right, Sterling stabbed his fork into his ham with merciless strikes. Pausing his attack, he tapped his index finger to it, as if trying to resuscitate the lump of meat.

Twitch developing behind my eye, I gave him a sideways glare. "If you keep playing with your food, I'm going to take it away."

Aghast by the mere thought of simply eating, Sterling stabbed a hand at the window. "The goose *flew away*!"

No valid counter argument for that existed. "Very well. Carry on."

Finished with his meal, Harwood wiped his face and tossed the napkin on his emptied plate. "Come, boy. Do the ole captain a favor and come have a look."

Casting a look of longing to the plethora of desserts he had yet to enjoy, Phin obediently shoved his chair back from the table. Behind my eyes I saw him as I had in the mirror — dead and putrefied.

My hand shot out before I could plan my next move, and I caught Phin's shoulder to hold him back. My every instinct prepared to put myself between him and the captain by any means necessary. "The boy has no business with the mirror."

A blink and Harwood's glare gleamed with reptilian hunger. Another, and it was gone quick as it came. "Is there a problem of some sort?" he asked, kind as you please.

Guiding the lad back into his seat with a firm insistence, I addressed the captain with my helmet of diplomacy firmly in place. "We were warded before departing on our journey. Prepared for that very mirror, in a manner of speaking. If anyone would see anything in it, it would be Sterling or myself."

Head slowly swiveling at the mention of his name, Sterling's lips parted with a pop. "The uninformed must improve their deficit or die?"

"Not quite to that extreme." I said, and patted his hand. "Eat your biscuit."

With a blissful smile, he obliged.

Fingers combing over his beard, Harwood leaned back in his chair to consider me through narrowed eyes. "In what way were you *prepared*?"

I brought my hands together before me, laced my fingers, and rested them on the table's edge. "King Liam employed a High Priestess to enchant us with particular attributes. Hence me being able to manifest things in this realm, and Sterling … bringing food to life."

"*Hades' wrath! Did it happen again?*" Palms slapping to the table, Sterling frantically scanned the entrees. After breathing a sigh of relief that everything was as it should be, he returned to buttering his biscuit.

"Is that so?" Steepling his fingers, Harwood brought them to his lips. "How fascinating."

"It is indeed." Sating my nervous thirst with a swig from my own stein, I offered the captain a forced smile. "That said, if you'd like me to have a look at that mirror, if would be my honor."

Before I could shift to move, Harwood halted me with the lift of one finger. "Tell me, what assurance have I—if that *is* the case—that you won't take what you need from the mirror and leave me near death and wanting?"

"I have no reason to keep anything from you." Bumping my newly appointed counterpoint with my elbow, I jerked my head in the captain's direction. "And you, Sterling?"

"Often, I find myself distracted when I should be productive," he stated around a mouthful.

"We'll take that to mean the same."

"I'm afraid that's just not enough of a certainty for me." Chewing on his lower lip, Harwood drummed his fingers against the tabletop. "I need a guarantee of answers … or one among you won't make it out of this room alive."

CHAPTER EIGHTEEN

W hat's this then?" I rumbled, limbs tensed for battle.

"Oh!" Sterling erupted, stabbing one arm in the air and shaking it wildly. "I know! It's a threat!" Leaning in my direction, he dropped his voice to a helpful whisper. "I get this a lot, it's most *definitely* a threat."

"Thank you, I noticed." Glower never shifting from the captain, my lip curled into a snarl. "What I don't know is *why*?"

Elbows propped on his armrests, Harwood wagged one finger in my direction. "Careful with the tone, boy. We don't need any reptilian visitors to tarnish our perfectly pleasant evening."

Feeling Phin tense beside me, his hand instinctively wandering to the wood flute nestled on his lap, I stifled the flames of my swelling rage down to a containable smolder.

"We agree to your ..." I choked on the loathsome word forming on my tongue, "*terms*, and you allow us the time and opportunity to get our questions answered as well."

A wry smile turning up the corners of his lips, Harwood attempted a mask of mock innocence. "I see no reason why not."

Be it coincidence, or intentional, Malyn picked that moment to clear her throat.

Taking it as a sign, whether she meant it as such or not, I scanned the room. Casually as I could, I searched for items that could be used as weapons if the need arose for us to fight our way off the ship. "Then, we proceed as men of our word."

"Splendid!" Harwood chirped, with a surprising spark of energy for someone so decrepit. "Let's not waste another second. Come 'round the table, lad, let's find out how to trap the crocodile once and for all."

Knot of dread tightening in my gut, I resigned myself to having no other options and pushed my chair back. As I skirted around the table, the clomps of my boots were the only sound echoing through the room. I kept my chin to my chest and eyes down as I walked, waiting until I was in position before that infamous artifact to gaze upon it. Settling into an easy stance, I shook out the tension in my arms … and allowed myself to peer into the unfathomable.

There was no time to fear I hadn't the gift for it. Upon first glance, I sank beneath the surface of its still façade. Breath slammed from my lungs, I found myself free falling in a pit of darkness. A minute or an hour later, I collapsed on the floor of a modest dwelling. Rolling onto my back, I greedily sucked in the air knocked from me. The home I found myself in had toys scattered across the room, and the smells of dinner filling the air. Sloppy slashes and splatters of blood covered every wall, dripping from the furniture and maliciously marring the happy family front. Which each inhalation the air's coppery taste burned down my throat.

In the midst of the carnage, a young and robust version of Captain Harwood flopped into a chair at the dining table. Gore-painted boots clomping down on the tabletop, he pulled a flask from inside his coat and slammed it back with an appreciative gulp. He cared not for the body sprawled at his feet, her blood-crusted auburn hair fanned around her slumped head. Nor the second, a man with thick waves of ebony hair, pinned against the wall by three swords run through his core.

In the doorway from the back hall, a face appeared. A sweet silhouette of untarnished purity blinked impossibly long lashes at the violence splayed out before her. She was an angelic girl of no more than five, who didn't cry out for her mama or papa. Crippled by shock, the shattered cherub could only stare. Stare at her fallen mother. Stare at her dangling father. Stare at the stranger oblivious to her presence who sat in her father's chair after destroying her world.

Jerked from that horrific scene, I was thrust back into the dizzying nothingness. My quaking knees threatened to buckle, but … were they holding me at all? Here, I had no limbs. No matter that mattered. Once again, the world settled with stomach lurching force.

Flames licked and hissed around me, yet I felt neither their heat nor burn. I was untouchable, unlike the poor souls screaming and crawling in hopes of escape. Robed figures darted in every direction, their panicked paths zigzagging in frantic quest for freedom. When hope for a reprieve by earthly means failed them, the figures dropped to their knees and uttered desperate prayers to Mount Olympus. Only then did my sinking heart grasp the truth; I was in a convent. Each member of the trapped cluster wore a lightning bolt medallion fastened over their heart to proclaim themselves faithful followers of Zeus. These were Sisters of the Mountain.

No sooner did I place them, then the side door burst open. Convinced their god had heard them, the sisters scurried toward this act of mercy. In place of divine intervention, Harwood and his crew sauntered in through a cloud of billowing smoke.

Eyes blurring with tears, the sister closest to the door didn't see the captain's pistol until it pressed to her temple. A thunderous blast sliced through the hall, and her lifeless form crumbled to the ground.

The other nuns tried to scatter, but found nowhere to hide. Captain and crew laughing in sickening sport, they raised their weapons. Shots rang out. Body after body fell.

Somewhere in the funnel cloud of chaos, Harwood found himself face-to-face with a young nun. Something about her struck a note of familiarity with him he couldn't quite place. Unlike the others, she didn't run, scream, or even try for the door. She simply stared. Stared as if she could see every vile thought that filled his head and wouldn't stop until she avenged each and every one.

Assuming a wide-legged stance, he swung the barrel of his gun to her forehead.

She didn't shrink away, but raised her chin in acceptance of his despicable nature.

The two locked eyes.

Harwood cocked his pistol.

Face vacant of emotion, she blinked at the devil before her.

The desire to bring her to her knees wafted from him in heady waves. Even so, he saw that something dark writhing in the pools of her stare; a beast of brimstone and wrath that seemed capable of weighing his every sin and judging him in righteous fury.

Dropping his pistol to his side, he hollered over his shoulder to his men. Without so much as a glance back, he fled the chapel, leaving a stilled storm of bedlam in his wake.

Still, the girl stared.

Yet again, my essence was hurled farther into the looking glass. This landing thrust me into the center of a makeshift village, comprised of shanties, wagons, and lean-tos. Every structure was eerily vacant, a scattering of bullet holes and cannon blasts blown through walls hinted at the horrific tale that had unfolded.

Spinning at the sound of approaching footfalls snapping through branches, I found a hodgepodge band of rum-soaked pirates stumbling out of the foliage.

"Cap'n?" the one leading the pack, with an eye patch and missing teeth, called into the camp.

"Where'd he get off to?" the stick of a man behind him asked, rising up on tiptoe to see over the brush and saplings.

"Saw that maiden that's been haunting him, he did," a third among them slurred, catching his stumbled steps by hooking a hand on a tree trunk. "Went running off in search of her."

Harwood picked that moment to appear, bursting from one of the wagons with the force of an enraged bull. Nostrils flaring, his heaving chest rose and fell in frenzied agitation. "She was here! I saw her!"

Shifting on their feet, his men exchanged nervous glances in their silent deliberation over which among them would speak on their behalf. When none among them volunteered, Patched Eye was shoved forward by the other two.

"Cap–Captain," he stammered, hands anxiously twisting together. "You claim to see this mysterious lass at every port, yet the men and I have never laid eyes on her. Is there a chance ..."

Harwood's head whipped around, daggers of murderous rage stabbing in the direction of the insolent bilge rat that would dare speak against him.

Stare drawn over his captain's shoulder, the pirate's one good eye widened in disbelief. "… that she's standing right behind ya?"

Harwood tensed, as if feeling the prickle of her presence, and slowly turned on the heel of his boot. She stood no more than an arm's distance from him.

The nun.

The raven-haired child with a forest of lush lashes, all grown up.

"You followed the path I left for you, Captain Harwood." Taking a brazen step closer, the harsh punch of her tone could have hammered spikes into a timber to string him up. "Accolades, for those are the last kind words I will *ever* speak of you and your miserable black heart."

Movement rustled all around. Members of the Roma camp appeared on every rooftop and surrounded the pirates from all sides. Dressed in flowing fabrics of every color, they were adorned with shiny bangles and hoops, and armed with an impressive assortment of weapons. Everything from slingshots to pistols were pointed at the slack-jawed crew, who had fallen right into their trap.

Seemingly oblivious to the shift in power, Harwood bubbled with giddy delight. "She's here! Can you see her? Tell me you all can see her!" the captain demanded of his crew.

"Oh, we can see her." The fumbling drunk staggered in a circle, blinking hard to focus on the coming fight. "And we see him, and her … with *that*, and … them with some sort of nightmarish pointy contraption."

"Spirit, *speak*!" Harwood boomed, throwing his arms out wide as if he were communing with the dead. "Why must you haunt me?"

Tilting her head, waves of ebony hair swayed to her waist. "You think me a ghoul, yet can't fathom why I would torment you? Do you claim to have led a virtuous life? That the blood of many doesn't stain your hands, and tarnish your soul with the filth of an oil slick?"

Arms swinging slack at his sides, he humored her claim with a snort of laughter. "Many have committed atrocities far more vile than I. Why dub me the villain?"

With a glance to her rooftop brethren, the girl planted her feet before him. "I was barely out of swaddling clothes, when you left me stewing in my parents' blood. Can you provide a word more fitting for such a man? Perhaps *diavol* is more fitting? It translates to *devil*."

Tipping his chin, Harwood peered up at her from under his brow, a sly smile twisting back one corner of his mouth. "It's vengeance, then? Shall we play it to the death?"

Cued by the promise of violence, his men pulled their swords in a menacing hiss.

Not an ounce of intimidation marred the girl's exotically beautiful features, she brought her hands together over her head in a sharp clap.

Her clan moved in response as one unified unit. Each lifted their right foot, and brought it down in a forceful stomp. To that, the earth itself answered their call to war. A wall of dust and leaves swelled from the ground, cocooning the captain and his accuser in a cell of nature's choosing.

Finding myself on the outside of the blockade, I simply stretched my essence to pop my way through.

Within, I found Harwood scanning his prison with mild interest and nonexistent alarm. "How is this done?"

"This is what your kind would call *gypsy* magic." Turning her head, the girl spat on the ground as if ridding herself of the foul taste left by such a word. "In reality, it is the strength of the Roma people rallied in a way you couldn't begin to fathom."

Hooking his thumbs in his belt, Harwood rolled his shoulders back in an easy stance meant to taunt her. "Gypsies, are ya? Then I encourage ya to drop this little act before you get yourself hurt, lass. I've traveled enough to know the only magic your people can conjure is of the smoke and mirrors variety."

Her head twitched in an avian fashion, eyes widening with manic rage. At the second jerk, an invisible hand closed around Harwood's throat. Clawed fingers grappling for freedom from the unseen force, his face transitioned from red, to purple, to blue.

"Does *that* seem like a sleight of hand?" she snarled. "Or would the sensation of the life being choked out of you convince you further?"

"What ... do ... you ... want?" Harwood gasped, watering eyes sending tears streaming over his cheeks.

"I want my parents back. I want my awakening into a world tainted by violence not to have come at such a tender age." As she spoke, she rolled her fingers into a fist and blew a gentle breath over her knuckles. "I want not to have spent the majority of my years tracking you down, and honing my skills to lure you to me. Most of all, I don't *ever* want you to scar another innocent soul as you did mine."

Her hand opened to reveal the embryo of a crocodile balanced on her palm. From nose to rump it was no more than the length of a finger, yet already its tiny snout sniffed at the air. Bulbous black eyes battled the heavy blinks of sleep. Its tail, still in the transparent portion of development, curled in to its body to show off newly acquired spots.

Raising her free hand, she brushed one finger over the croc's delicate skin. "The blood was so thick, it splattered up my ankles with each step. Not knowing what else to do, I curled up next to my mother's lifeless body until help came." Her stare, black with rage, shifted to Harwood. "It took two days. Their bodies had begun to swell with stink."

With a delicate touch, she brought the fetus to Harwood's cheek and cradled him there. Her wee cargo's snout twitched, rustling in the coarse hair of Harwood's beard. The pirate recoiled as much as the force holding him would allow. Drawn closer by the warmth, the croc nosed upward, moving in the direction of Harwood's bulging eye.

Harwood could manage little more than choked gasps as the croc wiggled into the corner of his eye socket, and began burrowing into his skull. Muscles spasming, his arms and legs locked out straight, shock setting in. As the last glimpse of the spotty tail disappeared behind the captain's eye, the girl released him. Slumped to the ground, he screamed his lungs raw. Digging at the back of his head, Harwood ripped his hair out in chunks as he felt every wriggle of the critter within.

All the while, the girl lorded over him, watching with hypnotized interest. "Your passenger will not take your life. He will not harm you or cause you any further pain ... unless you plot, scheme, or attempt to commit *any* malicious atrocity. If you do, he will burst forth and stop you in a magnificently grand display." Lifting the hem of her skirt, she crouched down beside Harwood to breathe against his ear, "Know this; every time he is called forth — each situation that demands he intervene — he will leave a bit more of himself behind until there's nothing left of you, at all."

Forcing his head up, Harwood's red-rimmed eyes pleaded for mercy. "Every curse can be broken! Please, speak of the key that will unshackle me from this prison!"

"Years I have spent preparing this punishment and tolling over the intricate details. What makes you think I would offer such a prize so easily?"

Gritting his teeth, Harwood tried to lunge for her throat, only to be halted by a lightning bolt of pain rocketing through his brain. One eye rolled skyward, the other squeezed shut. The left side of his face locked in a spasm. After a beat it passed, leaving Harwood on his hands and knees panting.

"Because," he croaked, "you're proud of the brilliance of your creation. You long to watch my face when I learn of the impossible terms to my release."

A victorious smirk morphed her enchanting features into a mask of wicked glee. "Of that, you are absolutely correct."

Fingers curling into the dirt, Harwood's head sagged to his chest. "Go on, then. Drive the nails farther into my coffin."

Reaching over, the girl pinched his chin roughly between her thumb and forefinger and forced his gaze to meet hers. "There is a mirror buried in a cave at the base of the Mytikas Peak. This mirror is said to hold the answers to all. But … in order to access such pivotal information, you must rely on that which you stole from me. *The pure and innocent heart of a child.* Only one fitting that description can access the mirror's truths. Even so, getting a young one to agree will become increasingly difficult as your appearance becomes more frightening. How can a child be expected to care for a creature contrived from their nightmares?"

Leaning in, at a proximity reserved solely for the most intimate acts of love or war, the girl peered not *in* to Harwood's eyes, but *through* them. Her chin tipped one way, then the other in search of… something.

"Shhh, shhh, shhh," she soothed the reptile within. "I can hear the flutter of your rapid heartbeat. Follow the sound of my voice, my son. Show your majestic face to me." In a sing song melody, she trilled, *"The hands of the clock have slowed to a stop, calling forth my tic-toc croc."*

I witnessed the captain's transformation once before. That experience could not compare to the virgin transformation. Harwood's scalp split down the center, ripping away to allow forth an eruption of emerald scales. Anguished screams tearing from his throat, Harwood's flesh shredded from his bones, allowing the crocodile to swell and surge to full towering height. Massive chest rising and falling, the croc blinked hollow black eyes down at his creator.

Hair sweeping over the small of her back, she tipped her head with maternal pride. Closing the distance between them, she pressed one palm to his cheek and smiled as the croc leaned in to her tender touch.

"My darling boy," she cooed. "You *are* the good in him. Give no quarter. Break him ... if you must."

CHAPTER NINETEEN

C"an you see anything?" Captain Harwood asked, eagerly perched on the edge of his seat.

The sound of his voice yanked me from the mirror, the world within the looking glass soaring past my ears in a deafening scream. Jarred back into reality, I blinked his way in my struggle to make sense of it all. "I was starting to."

Sucking air through his yellow-stained teeth, Harwood raised his shoulders to his ears, playing the part of a naughty little boy. "Apologies, friend. I'm merely an anxious old man."

Moments ago, I would have believed him. Now, I could see the darkness lurking behind his eyes. This was the same black-hearted man who treated himself to a drink while surrounded by the bodies of his victims.

"Can I get back to it, then?" was the closest I could manage to a cordial response.

"Aye, of course! Have at it." Waving me back toward the mirror, his shirt sleeve drifted up to reveal a glimpse of the scaled flesh scarring his forearm.

Filling my lungs, I peered into the glass once more.

Slightly more prepared for the punch of vertigo, this voyage landed me on the quarterdeck of the Jolly Roger. Midday sun beating down, the ship bobbed with the rolls of the current.

On deck below, a younger version of Potchis tended to his duties as a deck-hand by giving the floor a good mopping. Seeing him hard at work, the two lads who were supposed to be acting as lookouts in the crow's nest climbed down, determined to poke a bit of fun. One snatched the mop from his grasp. The other knocked him to the ground. Palms scrapped bloody by the deck boards, Potchis rolled onto his hip with his face blooming a bright carnation pink. Laughing until their sides ached, his tormentors plopped the wet mop onto his head. With the braided ropes dripping filthy water down his face and neck, they made kissy noises and told the mortified child-giant what a pretty girl he was.

Harwood watched all of this from his perch beside the mast, his lips curled in disgust at the weakling he had allowed aboard his ship. Clear as my own thoughts, I knew what he was thinking, and it twisted my stomach. Harwood toyed with the idea of tossing the boy overboard with a ball and chain clamped on his ankle. His sick rationalization? To spare the ship from having one more useless mouth to feed. No sooner did he entertain the revolting thought than a guttural growl of warning rumbled from his chest … the crocodile making its presence known.

Face falling slack, Harwood rolled his shoulders to shake off the onslaught. Even so, the warning did not go unheeded. Slapping his hands to the railing, he bellowed to the tyrants, "Leave him be! Part of the crew, he is!"

Begrudgingly, the men obeyed. Openly sneering in his direction, they tossed the mop at Potchis as he scrambled to get his feet under him.

The young lad was not familiar with such acts of kindness. No one had ever even cared enough to give him a proper name, or identity. Peering up at Captain Harwood, light haloing his formidable frame, the lad believed him to be a hero and thought himself most fortunate to serve under him. "Part of the crew, he is," he appreciatively parroted, and bowed his head to his captain.

Only I saw the cringe of distaste that stole across Harwood's face to have to address the boy. Or, heard the lone pop of flesh that straightened his spine and forced the captain to offer the lad a forced smile of acceptance.

A show of kindness … demanded by a monster.

Yet again, the mirror transported me in a blur. This time, I settled in the captain's quarters I had been pulled from. In brain-aching confusion, I watched *myself* arguing with Harwood. No such argument had happened. Yet, there Sterling was seizing my arm and tugging me away from the looming figures growing from the shadows to seize us both. A scream tearing from his narrow chest, Phin sprinted for the door. Moving with shocking agility, Harwood grabbed the dagger from my hip and lunged for Phin, catching him by the wrist. Before the crocodile had time to appear, Harwood carved into Phin from throat to sternum and ripped the still beating heart from his chest.

I came to in a blink, staring at nothing more than my own reflection in the surface of the gilded mirror.

"What did you see?" Harwood pressed in breathless anticipation.

Having crept up beside me somewhere along my journey, Sterling jabbed me in the ribs with his elbow. "Nothing except our own debonair reflections, aye?" Blinding terror drained his complexion waxen, his glowing jade eyes bulging. It seemed I wasn't the only one the mirror showed truth to. Whether it was the same grisly scenes or not, I could only hope to live long enough to inquire.

Placing my hand over his, I dipped my head in a nod of understanding, then turned my focus to the captain. "What you are plotting will not work. Even if the pure heart dies, your curse will hold." I could hardly recognize the voice that slipped from my lips. The velvet eloquence of its absolute certainty was foreign to my own ears.

A cloak of deathly silence descended.

Casting his gaze to the floorboards, Harwood's lips parted with a smack. "There's no denying reality sways in fickle ways here on Marooner's Rock. The improbable can be manipulated to bend the boundaries of the imagination. Even our own shadows can turn against … or become our strongest ally."

Light shifted behind me, the darkened corner suddenly coiling to life. Called forth from the flickering lantern overhead, Harwood's shadow stretched and grew toward the ceiling in an ominous black fog. Roiling and churning, it doubled in width then split down the middle into two faceless apparitions equally matched in size and intimidation.

Pressing both fists to his mouth, Sterling muffled a whimper. "I've often seen a man without a shadow. But never a shadow without a man. That may be the most curious thing I have ever seen, and I once beheld the brilling and slithy toves of a Jabberwock."

Arms raised defensively, as if I had the slightest notion how to fight what wasn't there, I grumbled under my breath, "I pray those aren't the last words I ever hear."

Bounding off the floor, one of the shadows flew straight for me. The misty wall of its influence slammed into my gut before I could swing to stop it, forcing the air from my lungs in a huff of pain. Driving me back, the faceless black mass cracked my head against the wall and pinned me there. I flailed against it, yet found myself no match for its strength. The dark nothingness of its forearm pressed to my throat, dragging me up the wall until the toes of my boots scuffed the floor. Eyes watering while I kicked for freedom, I saw out of the corner of my eye that Sterling was fairing no better than myself. He was bent in half and gasping for air, the other shadow holding him in an unyielding chokehold.

Heart thudding against my ribs, I cast my desperate stare to Phin. The lad clutched his flute tight to his chest, inching toward the door. Malyn and Potchis hovered behind him, yet neither moved to stop him. The mirror had not showed me where their allegiance would fall in the life of an innocent child, and the gamble of their favor was not one I was prepared to risk.

"Run." Choking on the word, I pulled back from the shadow as far as its grip would allow. Ignoring the pain crushing against my windpipe, I gulped in what little air I could and screamed, "*Now, Phin, run!*"

Finally spurred to action, he pivoted on the ball of his foot and bolted for the door.

Despite elements changing, so much of the scene was playing out just the same. The world slowing to a crawl, I turned my head in Harwood's direction, knowing full well I would see him shove his chair back with surprising might and lunge for the boy with his scaled hand outstretched.

Catching Phin's collar, Harwood spun him around.

A flash of silver.

A forceful grunt.

An echoing scream.

Mouth falling slack, Phin dropped his chin to his chest to gape at the sword run through his middle. Blood dribbling from his lips, a crimson bloom of gore sprouted on the front of his shirt.

"*Captain, what have you done?*" Potchis fell out of form to rush for the lad, only to be halted by Malyn's hand slamming against his chest.

"Stand down, Soldier!" Bellowing the command, Sergeant E'toil's voice betrayed her by cracking.

While the two scuffled, I was struck by a jolt of revelation. Letting one hand fall to my side, I slapped at my hip to confirm it. Yes! Harwood had stabbed Phin with his sword, meaning my dagger was still in my possession. Snagging it in an overhand grip, I brought my hand up fast and hard, driving the blade into the shadow's arm. The moment the steel made contact, his limb evaporated to a stump. Recoiling, the creature pushed back, sending me slumping to the ground and wheezing.

Gulping down a crucial breath, I utilized the blessing gifted by the mirror. "*The hands of the clock have slowed to a stop, calling forth my tic-toc croc!*"

Head whipping my way, Harwood's lip retracted into a snarl. "*No!* How could you know tha—"

Before the captain could finish his outraged revolt, the croc rolled his neck to shed the skin of his captor. In a grisly chorus of sight and sound, the beast molted as far as his shoulders. It was then he noticed his own hand piercing the chest of a child. Aghast at the sight, an anguished yelp escaped him. Offering the only solution the primal functions of his brain would allow, his lips curled from his lengthening fangs. Bone-crushing jaws parted, saliva dripping from each razor-sharp point. Arching back, he drove his head down, sinking his teeth into the wrist of his own offending limb. Blood sprayed, splattering the wall in heavy droplets. Eyes rolling back, the croc thrashed his head from side to side. Hard clamped teeth sliced through flesh and tendons. Tissue shredded to bone. A gruesome *thunk* and his amputated hand fell to the ground ... the fingers still twitching.

Head thrown back in a roar, the croc rescinded. Harwood came shrieking back into reality. Choking on his own tongue, he clamped his wrist to his chest while blood gushed from the severed stump.

CHAPTER TWENTY

The captain's grasp being all that had held him up, Phin's knees buckled beneath him. A silent scream frozen on his lips, the boy crumbled to the ground in a heap.

Scrambling to my feet, I shoved the reeling captain aside. I slid on my knees, catching Phin a second before his head could slam against the floor. A rush of air warned of the shadow's counter attack. Gritting my teeth, I curled my upper body around Phin, prepared to endure any onslaught to keep him safe. Eyes squeezed shut, I braced for a strike that never came. My lids popped open at the sounds of a scuffle. Potchis had shoved his way past Malyn and was wrestling the ominous void of a beast back. Weaving between the fracas, I rounded the table to where the mirror now lay across the remnants of the lunch spread. I pressed one elbow to its gold-leaf frame, shifted Phin's weight into one arm, and reached for Sterling with the other.

"*Get us out of here!*" I boomed, hoping the slight contact with the mirror would be enough to transport it along with us.

Crouching beside her captain, Malyn quickly wrapped his wrist with table linens to stop the bleeding. One wrong move struck an exposed nerve, earning an ear-piercing scream from Harwood. Good hand shooting out, he shoved Malyn back hard enough to send her tumbling. Her back swept the legs out from under the shadow holding Sterling, dissipating them into writhing black tendrils.

The apparition's grip loosened for a beat, and Sterling threw himself at the opportunity. Flinging all his weight forward, he grappled his way free and seized my outstretched hand.

The world beginning to strobe around us in a deafening pulse, Potchis' fray pitched him in our direction. Strength waning, Phin's limp hanging hand rolled back to catch hold of the gentle giant's shirt sleeve.

The nauseating pull of Sterling's "jump" matched that of a riptide. Unlike a vengeful current, this journey had little chance of ending in the jaws of a carnivorous sea monster, but a slightly elevated risk of winding up with my own head stuffed up my tail.

The earth rose to greet us in a merciless punch, hammering the breath from my lungs. Phin's shoulder bounced against my chest. Head lolling to the side, his eyes rolled back. A vise grip of fear closed around my heart at the blue tinge stealing over his lips. A *flump* beside me, and the mirror settled into the tall grass.

Our location? That part remained a mystery.

"You need to get the thorn out and stop the rushing waters," a strained voice offered from above. Tilting my head, I jerked to find Sterling dangling by his leg—his boot firmly lodged in the Y of two splitting branches. If I was deciphering his ramblings correctly, he was looking past his own unpleasant predicament out of concern for Phin.

Gently rolling on to my side, I eased the lad into the grass to evaluate his wounds. Harwood's sword jutted from his gut, his teeth chattering with the chill of blood loss.

"Where's the big guy? I could use another pair of hands." Fingers trembling over the polished silver hilt, I tried to recall my emergency training under the Royal Guard. Soldiers taking a stingray barb to the chest wasn't unheard of, I had seen it before and had even aided in the treatment. Even so, that was injury *in the sea*. There, bubbling blood evaporated in an instant, staining the current with a tang of rust that was quickly washed away. Here, it covered everything with sticky gore, its coppery stench gagging me.

Face reddening, Sterling turned his head in one direction then the other, searching the landscape for Potchis. "I don't see him. He may not have made the trip with us."

Tugging my shirt over my head, I balled the fabric into one fist. The other closed around the cold metal of the hilt. Filling my lungs, I exhaled through pursed lips. One steady yank. That's all I had to do. Pull the blade, then mash the fabric into the wound, and apply pressure to slow the bleeding. It sounded simple — a clear indicator it was not.

"*Run! You have to run!*" The shriek sliced through the moment like a scythe.

Hand jerking from the sword as if it had scalded me, my head snapped in the direction of the rustling brush and heavy footfalls.

Veins at his temples bulging, Sterling jabbed a finger to the north of us. "The big guy is coming in hot!"

Potchis crashed into view, waving his arms over his head. "*The captain! He's coming!*"

No sooner did his shout reach us than the Jolly Roger swelled over the valley. The entire massive ship was airborne, and sailing straight for us. Chains rolled and clinked, the menacing barrels of their weapons trained on us.

Arms falling limp, Sterling let them swing over his head. "I am really starting to hate this place."

At the first cannon blast, I dove for Phin. Mindful of the sword, I shielded his body. The ground shook, earth and rock showering us.

Thrown forward by the impact, Potchis crawled the remaining distance between us on his knees and elbows. "Is he okay?" he yelled to be heard over the ringing in his ears.

Two more blasts screeched through the air. One smashed through a tree in a spray of kindling, the other exploding a crater in the dirt.

"He won't be if your captain keeps shooting at us! *We need to move!*" Scooping Phin in my arms, I swiveled us out of the way as another blast caused the earth to buck in the space we vacated.

With a heave, Sterling folded himself in two and seized his pant leg. Frantically, he tugged for freedom. "*Let go, let go, let go!*"

Smoke and dust filled the air, each breath burning more than the last. Covering my mouth with the crook of my arm, I sought relief from the tainted air.

The sun disappeared overhead, blocked out by the bulkhead shadow of the Jolly Roger. Positioned at the helm, blood-soaked bandages wrapped the stump of Harwood's wrist. His remaining hand guided the vessel onward, hate radiating from his glare. Malyn lingered behind him, holding up a ticking clock to keep the croc at bay. Even then, minding the duties of her station, regret and concern crumpled her features. Harwood was the first person to ever show her kindness, even if it was all a ruse. I understood the loyalty she felt to him, and held no doubts she would question it from that day forward. Regardless, if I could find a way to blast him from the sky, I couldn't let myself hesitate simply because she was aboard.

"They were narrowly missing before," I stated, in between coughing jags. "Once they are directly over us, we don't stand a chance."

Potchis risked exposure by pushing himself up on to his knees, his stare locked on the gorge a meadow away from us. "I could carry him. If we could make it to the base of the gorge …"

I followed his gaze, over the wide-open space that led to the drop-off. "No matter how fast we run, we won't make it that far once they train their cannons. They don't need a direct strike. They can take us out by proximity."

"Someone throw a bloody rock!" Sterling swung back and forth, throwing his weight into the motion. "If it doesn't snap the branch maybe it will knock me out and spare me the initial anguish of having *my bits blown off!*"

Dragging a hand through my dust covered hair, I searched for an answer or ounce of hope. Inklings of both rasped from the lips of the fading lad cradled in my arms.

"*The rules … don't apply here. You … are … the Pan.*" Phin hadn't the energy to open his eyes, yet believed deeply enough to channel what was left of his depleting strength.

Chin jutting out with determination, I made it my solemn vow not to let that level of champion heroics be snuffed out. Easing the boy onto the grass behind a boulder to shield him, I drew my dagger and rose to my feet.

Sweeping my hand in Sterling's direction, I saw the branches parting to spill my trapped cohort to the ground, and so it was. He slumped to the earth with a grunt, then sprang to his feet. Swaying and disheveled, he blinked to focus while the world righted itself.

"Get the sword out of the boy," I demanded in a gruff tone that left no room for discussion. "And, *do not* let him die."

Hands clapped to his temples, most likely in hopes of steadying the roar of his pulse, Sterling dropped to his knees beside Phin. "What are *you* going to do?"

Brandishing the blade to the heavens, like my own sacred totem, my eyes narrowed. "The captain thinks he can fly."

Gathering Phin's hand in both of his, Potchis' nervous stare flicked in the direction of the floating ship. "He *can* fly," he pointed out.

Closing his hand around the hilt of the sword, Sterling paused. "Wait, *he* can fly?" he questioned, stabbing a thumb Harwood's way.

Glaring up at the Jolly Roger from under my brow, my voice dropped to a threatening growl. "Oh … he can *fly*."

In my mind I saw the ship changing course, rocketing from this land at speeds that knocked the crew to their knees. I didn't *suggest* the reroute. My will *demanded* it. Screeching to a stop, as if run aground by an unseen dune, the Jolly Roger repelled back. Gaining speed in its descent, shouts echoed from above. Bellowing his fury at the helpless crew, Harwood's neck snapped to an unnatural angle. In moments, the crocodile would appear to spare them all his venomous rage. They would be long gone by then. The only tug of regret I felt was for Sergeant Malyn, peering over the port rail in shock as Marooner's Rock disappeared beneath her.

Higher and higher they soared, the ship shrinking by the second. Until, at last, the tiny speck of it blinked from sight.

Arm falling to my side, a light chuckle of wonder escaped me. "*He flew.*"

CHAPTER TWENTY ONE

With no time to celebrate the victory, I bolted to Phin's side in the same instant Sterling began his countdown to heroism or tragedy. "One … two … three … *pull!*"

In one steady motion, he extracted the blade and tossed it aside. Blood gurgled up from the cavernous wound, seeping out around him in a crimson cloak. Plugging the gash with my bundled shirt, Sterling applied pressure in hopes of slowing the fatal bleed.

Focusing yet again, I willed it to stop. Commanded the spurting vessels to clamp shut. To my dismay, the blood continued to gush, forming an inky pool beneath Phin's slight frame.

"Come on, lad," I urged, eyes burning with the sting of my own failure. Pressing my hand over his heart, I prayed for a miracle … that didn't come.

Beneath my palm, his chest stilled.

His heart gave one last shuddered beat.

The world stilled, and a lifeless boy—who counted on *me* to protect him—lay cold in the grass.

Falling back on my heels, tears streaked my cheeks. "I failed him. He thought me a god, someone worthy of keeping him safe, and I …" head falling back, I watched the clouds of my anguish roll in, "failed."

"It seems not everyone received the telegram," Sterling mused, his inane rambling painted with a sorrowful pallet. "He wishes to play but knows not how."

"What are you on about?" I snapped.

Flinching at my gruff tone, Sterling merely pointed to the section of grass alongside Phin. It took me a moment to see it, having to wait for one of the clouds of my creation to pass. Then, there it was. Phin's shadow crouched by his boy, head tilted in search of a way to wake his playmate.

"Sterling, you're a bloody genius." Voice dropping to an urgent whisper, I drew my dagger once more.

"I'm in mourning," Sterling tsked, shaking his head. "There's no need for name calling."

Not taking the time to clarify or explain, I palmed my dagger and shifted to Phin's feet. Stabbing the point into the earth, I sawed his shadow free—much to its dismay. The faceless anomaly flailed and stomped in protest of my desperate act.

"Sorry, mate, greater good and all that," I offered in a paltry excuse. One final swipe and their connection was severed, the black vine of mist that had connected them now gripped tight in my fist. Hand over hand, I rolled the shadow in, a wispy rope that wound up my wrist with barely a whisper of a touch.

"We both care for him, and this is the only help I can think to give," I muttered in solace to the shadow. Careful as I could, I wadded it into a ball no bigger than an apple. It took both hands and a fair amount of force to jam the wriggling essence into the gaping pit in Phin's chest.

"Wh–what are you doing?" Potchis asked, a twinge of hope daring to creep into his tone.

"Acting on blind faith." Clasping both palms over the wound, I captured the shadow within Phin's vacant shell.

"I–I think I actually can help here," Sterling stammered, as if more startled by that realization than the rest of us.

"How?" I pressed as he edged up alongside me.

Placing his hands over mine, he gave me a sheepish side-smile. "If all goes well? We're going to bring a roasted goose back to life."

"That's the first time I understood one of your … musings," I pointed out. Wordlessly, I wondered what else he had seen in all his various jumps, and if it all gave merit to his seemingly incoherent mutterings.

"Terrifying, isn't it? Now," he jerked his chin in Phin's direction, "*focus.*"

Working elbow to elbow, we trained all our energy and attention on young Phin. Behind my eyes, I saw his wound closing, felt the shadow settling in to be the spark of life within the boy, pictured it all coming together to bring him back.

The moment dragged on long enough to exhaust optimism.

Then …

Phin bolted upright, eyes wide with fright. Gulping air in frantic pants, his gaze traveled over each stunned face staring down at him. Clawed hands scraping my arm, he gripped my shirt sleeve in a white-knuckled panic.

Scanning the blood-soaked grass, I searched for that which acted as his life preserver in the treacherous waters of life. "His wood flute! *Where is it?*"

"Here, sir! It's here!" Potchis scrambled over on hands and knees, retrieving the instrument from where Phin lost hold of it.

Accepting the treasured artifact with a nod of thanks, I offered it to the bewildered boy.

Phin took it without comment or question, his fingers instinctively tracing over the letters etched in the side. A million questions had to be racing through his young mind, yet the first that tumbled from his lips stunned me. "You saw something … within the mirror."

My gaze settled on the golden frame nestled in the grass.

"I did," I admitted, dragging my tongue over my bottom lip. "Unfortunately, it wasn't enough to keep you out of harm's way."

Chin falling to his chest, the look that stole over the lad's features held a wisdom far beyond his years. "My memory is foggy," he confessed, index finger tracing over the letters engraved in his instrument. "I remember my mother's face, and the feel of the sword running me through. Yet I can't recall my last day at the castle, or how it was we came to be here."

"Cling to your flute, as I have my stone." Turning my palm skyward, I showed him the rock infused with the Ice Queen's tear still tied there. While it didn't possess the same sting on Marooner's Rock, its chill each time I squeezed it reminded me of the cool waters of Atlantica. "Let it be your beacon of true north."

"P … T … R," he read off the flute. "I wonder how long it will be that I remember what it stands for?"

"I reckon until old age claims what's left of your memory." Bounding to my feet, I offered Phin a hand up. "Once we leave Marooner's Rock, a detached shadow will be the worry of another realm."

"Uh … Alastor?" Sterling interjected, raising one finger to catch my attention.

Placing his clammy hand in mine, Phin let me heave him from the ground. "And Harwood, how does he fair?"

"*The Pan* evicted him." A mischievous wiggle of my eyebrows earned a giggle from the lad as sweet as an angelic symphony. "We have nothing to fear from the dastardly pirate any time soon."

Rising to his feet, Sterling brushed the grass from his knees, then politely tapped me on the shoulder. "Alastor, this matter is quite an urgent one."

Perhaps it was my growing bond with the oddball, said to be my counterpoint, that had me dreading his words before he could utter them. I could feel the storm cloud of unease roiling within him. Keeping my expression at neutral for Phin's benefit, I offered Sterling my ear. "What is it?"

True heartache creases the brow with a valley of suffering. It crinkles the corners of the eyes in threat of tears to come. The chin crumbles, quaking with sobs ready to burst forth when the dam of emotion finally breaks. *This* is the story that was scrolled across Sterling's features, before he found the strength to speak the words. "He can't leave here."

Swallowing hard, I rasped, "Why?"

"Because the boy *died* here." Gnawing on his lip, Sterling searched for the right words to help me understand. "The magic keeping him alive here doesn't *exist* back in the realm we're returning to. If he leaves this land, he reverts back to the version of dead that *doesn't* hop back up and saunter around."

Trust the ever-insightful lad not to miss the shift in mood. "What's happened? Why do you both seem troubled?"

Filling my lungs, I rubbed my hand over the back of my sweat-dampened neck. Humidity clung to my skin, the air itself suffocating me. My gaze betrayed me by wandering to the mirror. Not in search of answers as much as one last lingering glance at Vanessa before I was forced to let the tides of fate tear us apart … forever.

Lips parting with a smack, my eyebrows raised in feigned acceptance of a course I could not change. "Well, it seems we won't be leaving here after all. Not if we want to keep you above the daisies, instead of feeding them." Bringing my hands together in a crisp clap, I forced a tight smile that I wager closer resembled a grimace. "Where shall we set up camp? I'd like to stay away from the mermaid lagoon, if it's all the same to you. Wherever we choose, we could scavenge through the camp of Harwood's crew for supplies and materials and make ourselves a rather posh abode."

Planting his feet in a wide-legged stance, Phin stabbed his hands onto his hips. "No," he demanded, with surprising conviction. "*I* will set up camp. *You* have a kingdom to return to."

Even as emotional exhaustion set in, the lad's efforts earned a hint of a smile from me. "I'm not going to leave you here, Phin. I'm a soldier that believes in honor and duty, and as such I would never desert one of my men. Especially when they're pint-sized."

"You haven't asked me where I was." The lad pointed out, kicking at the dirt with the toe of his moccasin.

Pulling back in confusion, I struggled to follow his conversational deviation. "Where you were? When?"

Head cocked, he peered up at me with a face of blatant truth. "I died, Alastor. You're not at all curious where I went?"

Flopping down in a clean section of grass, Sterling crossed his legs and focused his attention entirely on Phin. "I, for one, would *love* to know. I've been to no less than six realms I could have *sworn* were heaven, and I'd love to hear if any come close. Was there a shrine to pastries, or an excess of fluffy puppies? Those are the ones I'm hoping for."

Lifting his chin, a light breeze blew Phin's chestnut locks across the apples of his freckle covered cheeks. "I found my parents. For so long I've missed them and prayed to be reunited —"

Breath catching with regret, I squeezed my eyes shut for a beat. "And I pulled you away from them."

"Much to their *delight*," Phin corrected, not in sadness but conviction. "They were *heartbroken* to see me there so soon, Alastor. Our reunion was filled with their tears over what should have been. My presence sullied their utopia. Not because they don't love me, but because they wanted a long life for me full of adventure and experience. There's no reason that can't happen here."

How he had gained such strength of character so young, I couldn't fathom. When I was his age, my deepest thought was if manatees could be ridden. (They can, by the way. As long as the rider doesn't care where they are going, or if they ever get there.)

"You stay, we stay," I reiterated.

Hand on his knee, Sterling swiveled in my direction. "Pardon? Did you say *we*?"

Closing both hands around the flute, Phin shuffled through the meadow. His steps stilled when his toes brushed the mirror's frame. "And what of the queen? I can't recall her name, but I remember her to be kind and fair. Will you sentence her to death? That the sweet princess would be raised without her mother? They're counting on you, Alastor. Can you willingly disappoint them?"

"What I can't do is leave you alone," I countered, folding my arms over my chest. "You're a *child* … albeit an insightful one."

Pushing off the ground, Potchis rose to full height and brushed the grass from his palms. "He won't be alone. Boys need someone to look out for them. I will stay with him."

"You've been trapped here," Phin pointed out, face folding in a blend of appreciation and woe. "I couldn't ask that of you."

One hefty shoulder rose and fell in an easy shrug. "This is home," Potchis declared. "I could never leave this never-land."

"There you have it, then," Phin stated, the matter all but decided by his standards. "We have no need for either of you here. It's time for you to head back and be the heroes you are meant to be."

Before I could argue further, Sterling leapt to his feet and bounded around the edge of a neighboring boulder. "*Sometimes botany is the answer!*" he caterwauled as he vanished.

"I'm not sure if he's ever coming back," I admitted in the silence that followed.

A beat later, Sterling returned with the stem of a lone daisy clutched in his fist. Pausing alongside Phin, he nodded to the flute. "May I?"

Curious to see where this was headed, Phin temporarily relinquished his treasure into Sterling's care.

Tiptoeing around the blood splattered patches of earth, Sterling hummed a merry tune back to my side to present me with the flower. "Hold this, if you please."

"What do I do with it?"

Rapidly blinking his bewilderment, he tilted his head. "We're said to be connected, are we not? Two sides of the same coin. If such a thing is true, I would think you would know."

A chuckle brewed in my throat at the lunacy of such a concept. Yet it was something in Sterling's stare that snuffed out the laughter before it dared leave my lips. There was a plea held in the depths of his gaze, a desperate need to find truth in the implausible. That a connection had been forged to anchor him to someone, when too many others had floated in and out of his erratic existence.

Did I have any idea what he was asking of me? Not in the least. Even so, he needed the kindness of an attempt, and that I would not deny him.

"I suppose it does." Dipping my chin in thanks, I accepted the flower.

Manic smile widening, Sterling flopped down in the grass and brought the flute to his lips. I recognized the tune he played at once, it being the same melody he used in the courtyard to call forth the woodland nymph.

Maybe it *was* the bond that fused us together, maybe it was chance. But, in that moment, I knew without question what Sterling was asking of me. Cradling the wild flower in my palm, I let my thoughts whisk me back to the moment when that twinkle of light swirled into the creature of innocence and love that touched the heart of all those she encountered. With a laugh of sweet tinkling bells, she saw the scars on every soul and uttered the words needed to heal them. Magic I couldn't fathom responded to my musings. A spray of light swirled in my hand, causing the stem to twitch and roll. Eyes widening, my jaw swung slack as a figure formed within the daisy. The leaves became a gown to the minuscule beauty, the silky white petals waving into flaxen locks. Iridescent wings stretching from her back, she lifted the point of her chin up at me. Sky-blue eyes gleamed up at me, an angelic grin warming her face.

"Is that a fairy?" Voice dropping to an excited whisper, Phin's shoulders rose to his ears as he edged in closer for a better look.

"That she is, as well as being your very own homing pigeon, of sorts." At my rather unfavorable description, our new little friend stomped her foot in irritation. Acorn-sized face reddening, she expressed her discord in an aggravated chorus of chimes.

Stifling a laugh, I held up my free hand in retreat. "My apologies. You're right. That really wasn't a flattering comparison. How about this? They should consider you their stealthy communications officer, who has been gifted with the capabilities to travel between realms?"

A head nod and lone jingle acted as my confirmation of approval.

"Well, go on then," I encouraged, lifting my palm to chest level to give her a boost. "Go say hello."

Wings fluttering at hummingbird speed, she lifted from my hand. While Sterling's song faded, the fairy swirled around Phin's head. The lad's bark of laughter as he whirled to keep up with her soothed my troubled heart.

"I couldn't possibly leave without knowing you can reach out if need be." Fingers laced, I let my hands fall in front of me. "Our new friend can be the liaison to accommodate that very thing. If you find yourself in any trouble at all, send her to find me, and I will come straight away."

"We," Sterling corrected. Popping to his feet, he handed the flute back to Phin. "Good luck getting here without me."

Phin offered the fairy his arm to land on. She eased down gentle as a feather, her slight weight not causing his arm to dip in the slightest. With her happily settled, he glanced my way with a serene smile that seemed to hold ages of wisdom. "I suppose there's nothing left to hold either of you here. That means it's time for you to go and be champions for the others that need you."

Adjusting the belt tied around his middle, Sterling's jade stare swept the landscape. "It's probably best we do. It seems I've seen all there is here. You might not believe this, but when I get bored," leaning his shoulder into the center of our cluster, he dropped his voice to a whisper, "I go a bit mad."

"N–no one finds that hard to b–believe," Potchis stammered, blushing at his own brazen attempt at wit.

Spine snapping straight, Sterling rewarded him with a slow, deliberate clap. "I couldn't even begin to be insulted by that. Brilliantly executed."

Eyes rolling once more at his antics, I focused on Phin with a protective urgency that couldn't be misconstrued. "And you're *sure* you'll be okay?"

It was with great reluctance that Phin tore his gaze from the fairy prancing up and down his arm. His cheeks were the dusky rose of a boy smitten. "Potchis existed here long before we arrived. He can show me how to get food, and water. The camp site of Harwood's troop will give us everything we need to settle in comfortably."

Bobbing his head, Potchis snorted his agreement.

"Then, I suppose there's only one thing left to do." Closing my hand around the grip of my dagger, I let it hiss free from my belt and took a knee before the boy. As I held it up between us, I concentrated my essence. "Whatever power I hold in this realm, I grant to this dagger and he who wields it." Turning the blade toward my chest, I offered Phin the hilt. "Take it. *You* are the Pan now."

Face aglow with the light of a thousand candles, he accepted my offering with a tentative hand.

Tiptoeing across Phin's shoulder, the shimmering fairy's awe matched his own.

"It fits your grip perfectly." Voice gruff with emotion, I rose to my feet. "Far better than mine ever did. I always found it a bit snug. Now, I know why. It was meant for you from the moment it was forged."

With more gratitude than I knew a child capable of, the lad tilted his face to mine. "Thank you, to both of you, for all you have done for me. It seems greedy to want for more, yet I must ask one final favor before we part."

"Anything," Sterling granted, before I could voice the same declaration.

Phineas Theodore Rutherford blinked up at us with a youthful exuberance time would never squash. "If you encounter any other lost boys like us, send them here for a place they can call home."

CHAPTER TWENTY TWO

"Only once before have I *ever* regretted a jump this badly." Bent in half, Sterling muttered the sentiment to the dirt beneath his feet as he waited for the world to steady around us.

Trying to stand, I stumbled, swayed, then fell on my butt with a *huff*. "We have to trust they'll be okay. And if not, we armed them with their fairy emergency plan."

"That's only helpful if I can find my way back to their *exact* time, and space." Shaking off the effects of our journey far easier than I could, Sterling stretched out his back and offered me a hand up. "Maps to such are misconstrued, their keys ever-changing."

"We have to have faith that, if the need were to arise, their fey charge will be able to lead us right to them," I said in gentle reminder, and clasped his hand with mine.

The moment our palms touched, the vision of Sterling earning his facial scars punched behind my eyes, choking me on the violence. Squeezing my hand around my ice stone, I rolled away from him and retched the contents of my stomach onto a patch of wild daisies.

"Your sight is back?" Sterling hovered behind me, wanting to offer aid but unsure of quite how.

Heaving yet again, all I could manage was a meek nod.

"On a good note," he pointed out, his tone helpful optimism, "that proves we are definitely back in Caselotti, and no one's head is on upside down. These were both viable concerns I am thrilled to have overcome."

Hands on my knees, I inhaled through my nose and out through my mouth, fighting to calm my spasming gut.

"Stirring performance, boys. Truly, I held no doubt you'd return victorious." If I hadn't recognized Hades' slimy cadence, the three panicked gasps that followed—his body's reminder he had lungs—surely would have given him away.

Forcing myself upright, to the protest of my churning stomach, I wiped my mouth with the back of my hand. "Hades, were you prowling this realm, ready to pounce the very *instant* we returned?"

Back to the trunk of a Silk Oak tree, Hades pushed off and sauntered closer. A tilt of his head caused blue-black hair to brush his shoulders, his eyes narrowing. "I figure the moment you march within the castle walls toting your prize, you'll be swarmed with appreciative attentions. I needed a moment of your time before your heroes' parade can begin."

Curling one leg under me, I prayed to Mother Ocean the limb would support my weight, and tried to stand. Thankfully, it wavered but held. "You have another quest to send us on first?" Lip curling into a snarl, my words were venomous. "Another innocent child for us to watch die?"

"Is that what happened?" Pacing closer, Hades clasped his hands behind his back. "That must have been simply *dreadful* for you."

The malicious gleam swirling in the pools of his black stare led me to believe he knew far more about this particular topic than he let on. He was the Lord of the Underworld. Had young Phin swam in his sea of souls?

"Even so," he sighed with a slathering of indifference, "I merely requested you fetch the mirror. Any lives harmed as a result, were entirely *your* doing."

Hands curling into fists at his sides, Sterling's chest swelled with a fury I hadn't thought him capable of. "You bloody bastard." His response was punctuated by the crackle of splintering wood. A branch directly over Hades' head came careening down, straight on course for the demi-god. Its impact was thwarted by a cobalt blaze firing from Hades' palm. A blink and the bough was nothing but ash.

"Look whose trickster abilities are developing. That is a *very* good thing." Hades clucked his tongue against the roof of his mouth. "I'd watch that though. It seems to wreak *hell* on your complexion."

Hades' hand shot out a second time.

A scream ripping from his throat, Sterling clutched his face and folded to the ground.

"*What have you done?*" I demanded, kneeling beside my whimpering friend.

"Oh, he'll be fine." Hades brushed my concern aside with an elegant roll of his wrist. "The pain will pass in a moment. Then, he can live with the gentle reminder not to *threaten a god!*"

His declaration boomed around us, shaking the earth and echoing from every tree.

Trembling, Sterling's face rose to mine, tears streaking down his face.

"It burns," was all he could muster. Blue stripes had been branded into his skin, framing his face with the demi-god's wrath.

Throwing his arms up, Hades let them fall to his sides with a slap. "See, now we're getting all off track. I merely came with instruction on how to handle the mirror."

"Say what you will, and go!" I growled. Closing my hand around my stone to hinder a vision, I hooked Sterling's elbow and helped him to his feet.

"*Aw,*" Hades' face folded into a mock-pout, "and I *had* hoped we'd honor the sacred bond of former mermen. But, have it your way. My message is a simple one. King Liam wants the mirror. You mustn't give it to him. It is to be delivered to Queen Evelyn, and *no one* else."

"The king wishes to save his queen," I argued, fully expecting to be brandished with my own scars soon enough. "He's expecting—"

Shoulder's sagging, Hades' head fell back in exasperation. "*Ugh!* Olympus save me from the ignorance of mortals! The queen is already dead! *There is no saving her!*"

"But, we went for the mirror ..." Hearing that for the paltry excuse it was, my weak counterpoint died on my lips.

The sizzle of power pulsing over his skin, Hades edged in close enough for his presence to shrink mine. "Come now, do we really need to play this game? You have the sight, boy. You knew the fate of the enchanting queen before setting foot on Marooner's Rock."

"I thought there would be a way." In light of his revelation, the excuse sounded like the pathetic plea of a child. In retrospect, I suppose that's *exactly* what it was.

"Would it help if you knew what happened?" Hades' mouth screwed to the side, proof he was humoring me. "She was lured into an alley by a sweet song the night of your farewell feast. There, she found a towering beast, all vicious talons and ravenous jaws. Poor thing barely had a chance to scream before it devoured her."

It wasn't a fabrication. I had seen as much in a vision I chose to ignore, because it suited me.

Blue blaze igniting in the depths of his gaze, with the hitch of one brow Hades challenged me to look away. "The heels of her lace ankle boots thunked together, as the beast dragged her into the forest by her hair. His skin was covered with moss. One lone tusk protruded from his dramatic under bite. Big as he was, his weight was balanced on two narrow hooves like those on a cow or pig. He held no malice for the beloved queen, but acted only on the orders of his master. And, do you know who *that* would be?" Stepping in close enough for the stench of brimstone to burn my nostrils, Hades whispered against my ear, "She came to you after I gifted you with the sight. Visited you as the High Priestess cared for you, because she knew how important you were to her cause. Did you see it when you woke? The truth staring back at you, as if you'd been returned to the depths? A malevolent force hungry for revenge ... particularly against the woman *you* love."

"Amphrite?" Having no proof to back the claim, her name passed my lips as a lobbed guess.

Easing back a pace, a victorious smile twined across Hades' lips. "And look who's catching up. The former queen has been banished from the seas and the newborn babe she left behind. She holds Vanessa to blame, and is plotting her route to revenge. I seek to redirect her ... elsewhere."

"And what matter is it to you what happens under the seas?" I could feel the tension of the thread I was pulling at, yet had to know how the matter unraveled.

Wagging his finger in my direction, Hades strolled a slow circle around Sterling and myself. "I suppose there's no point in keeping up pretenses over the matter. No doubt when I left Atlantica after the death of Queen Titonis, Poseidon's first wife, I left behind plenty of fodder for rumors and whispers. Although, there's a chance you were too young to hear those crows of gossip."

"You asked to leave Atlantica after witnessing your own brother beaching his bride." Out of the corner of my eye, I saw Sterling trying to blink through his pain and confusion, and raised a hand to steady him. "No one could fault you that."

Shaking his head, Hades muttered under his breath, "If only it were that simple. Poseidon accused Titonis of having a human lover, with which she had conceived a child. Lost to his jealousy, he followed her to the shoreline and watched as she used the limited magics she had to walk on land and meet her love. For this, he condemned her to death. I tried to intervene. Injected the limited voice that I had as his alchemist. Even so, Poseidon's mind was made up. Titonis would die. Unable to watch such a tragedy unfold, I beseeched Mount Olympus to reassign me to any world, any realm, to spare me this barbaric display. To my great regret, Zeus did just that." Hades' steps stilled. Staring at the ground, his words came controlled and measured. "I took my place as Lord of the Underworld just as Titonis died. It became my job to usher the woman I loved, who *I* had been meeting on shore behind my brother's back, into the eternal pool that would later become the River Styx. All the while knowing I was impotent to save her." Pivoting on the ball of his foot, the flickering flames of Hades' stare burned into Sterling and I. "And who was it that whispered in Poseidon's ear about the possible betrayal? Who positioned herself to become queen to my brother, and step-mother to *my* child?"

Tentatively, Sterling dabbed at his stripes with the tips of his fingers. "I want to say Amphrite, but it seems such an obvious answer."

"She got Titonis killed, and in turn Vanessa banished her from her own child. It seems your *heir* has secured vengeance for you." Even as I spoke, I searched Hades' face for elements that tied him to Vanessa. Sharp cut cheekbones. Pointed chins. And, of course, their unimaginable power. While I could never feel the ties that bound her to Poseidon, they were tangible with Hades. He was ready to claim her, which was more than his brother had ever been willing to offer to the baby girl he had raised from birth.

A slow burn cast shadows of loathing across Hades' features that made him appear more demon than man. "That may have been the case, if it weren't for Amphrite's one … last … betrayal. I'm sure you have some inkling of what that was. You watched the ramifications of it play out on shore."

Tentacles of fear squeezed my heart, squeezing ink black fear pumping through my veins. "The merman."

"That's right." Wisps of sapphire steam licked across Hades' hunched shoulders, fueled by his rage. "She vowed to help Vanessa with the spell, then abandoned her once it had been evoked. *She* was to blame for their deadly transformations. Yet, *my daughter* was left to pay the price."

"What price?" Fear of the answer made the words burn from my throat.

To my surprise, the demi-god's features softened. "Dear boy, didn't you know? Vanessa endured the Kiss of the Kraken."

Five words, and I understood Hades' curse to be unable to breathe on dry land.

The Kiss of the Kraken. The ultimate punishment among my people. So feared was it, that few dared to speak of it. Beaching went for death. The Kraken's kiss was spawned in the deepest pits of pain and suffering.

"Is she—" I couldn't bring myself to utter the word. As if enunciating its syllables could bring about the unthinkable.

"Dead?" Hades prompted. Clapping his hands before him, he rubbed his palms together until azure sparks flickered from his fingertips. "Oh, no. She tried to die. I simply couldn't allow that. I denied her passage, and forced our girl to … *endure*. I'm afraid she will never again be the maid you once knew."

Legs failing me, I sank to a squat, my head cradled in my hands.

"Amphrite was the cause of that pain being inflicted on *my* child. Meanwhile, I—once again—was powerless to protect one I hold dear." Seemingly oblivious to my mental implosion, Hades paced a trench into the earth before us. "And I did care for her! If I had it to do all over again, I never would have left. I would have stayed, for Vanessa. Even if I couldn't announce myself as her father, I could have been there for her. So, she had *someone*."

Chin jutting out, Sterling bristled on my behalf. "She did have someone. She had *him*." His thumb jabbed in my direction. "Yet, you tore them apart just the same."

Hades' hand shot out in Sterling's direction, palpable ire crackling down his steaming forearm. Nostrils flaring, he forced the threatening limb to his side. "There was nothing he could have done short of watching the woman he loves be torn to ribbons. I *spared* him!"

Their words were a distant echo down a long hall — my mind locked in the prison of this newfound knowledge. Every thought was consumed with the anguish she must have endured as the venom coursed through her veins, attacking her body with its fatal poison.

"Now, this same villainous enchantress has taken Queen Evelyn's identity in her search for a way back to her own child. This..." flames licked up Hades' cheeks; with a roll of his neck, he was able to subdue them, "I can't allow. I—"

Snapped from the moment, his shoulders sagged.

"Are you listening? Is he listening? I'm not really feeling heard, here. And, if there's one thing I can't tolerate—"

Glaring up at him from under my brow, I pulled myself up to full height. "Amphrite is Queen Evelyn, and seeks the mirror. Why wouldn't you want me to keep it far from her grasp?"

"Because, dear boy," Hades purred with a devilish grin. "Far more fun can be had if you give it to her straight away."

"What in this is fun?" There was something Hades was leaving out of this. One remaining cog in the wheel that would glide us to his true intent. "Why would we help her, when we could give it to her husband so that he may vanquish the fiend who destroyed his family?"

"Aw," Hades pursed his lips like I had just graced him with the most adorable display he had ever witnessed, "you still think you're the heroes here. No, no, lad. You're glorified errand boys. You will give the mirror to Amphrite so that she may use it to get where I need her."

"And where is that?" I pressed.

Snapping a twig off a branch, Hades rolled it between his fingers. "Your time on Marooner's Rock surely must have showed you that powers, of any kind, work differently in various realms. I have found one in particular where I am my most rancorous self."

Sparks sizzled from his fingers, igniting the stick in an indigo blaze. "Twice the size of the land's twisted, towering trees, the beat of my spike-covered wings against the air drives the bravest of folks to their knees. Skin covered in emerald scales, a row of spikes trails down my spine."

A gasp seeping from his parted lips, Sterling stumbled back, eyes wide with fear. "The … Jabberwock."

Crushing the flames he created in his fist, Hades swung toward Sterling with a toothy grin. "You've heard of me. How fabulous."

"Can't go back! Don't make me go back!" Sterling pleaded, gaze lobbing in every conceivable direction in search of escape from ghosts of the past closing in. "Don't know where I'm going. Can't be lost. Not really here. Not really there. Beware the paint, or it's off with your head!"

"The mere mention of my name broke your friend," Hades snorted, gleefully biting his lower lip. "This is a strangely proud moment for me."

With a purposeful sidestep, I positioned myself between Sterling and the demi-god. "Give me one good reason we should involve ourselves in this matter at all, when it would be far easier to stand aside and let you rip Amphrite apart?"

The humor vanished from Hades' face, leaving behind a conniving chill. "Besides the fact that you swore fealty to me? I can think of three that answer to but one name."

"A reflection sometimes exposes more reality than the object it echoes," Sterling whimpered behind me.

Holding out one hand to calm him, I showed Hades no quarter. "I've seen your three-headed strumpet, and find myself far from intimidated."

"That's because you haven't seen what a bitch they can be." Sticking two fingers in his mouth, Hades blasted a loud whistle that resonated all around.

The forest itself seemed to answer his call. Branches snapped. Spooked birds took to flight. The ground quaked beneath our feet.

Arms locked out to his sides, Sterling blanched. "J-Jabberwock?"

Instead of clarifying, Hades taunted him with a wink.

Pushed to the limits of dread, Sterling's eyes rolled back, and he fainted dead away.

He was spared the jarring sight of Cerberus crashing through the tree line. Her feminine physique had been replaced by a lupine one that towered over us. Black coat gleaming, the three-headed wolf growled and snapped in ominous warning.

Striding to the side of his pet, Hades lovingly scratched her shoulder. "See what I did there? With the bitch comment? It was a fun play on words! Seriously, though, she'll tear your friend limb from limb if you don't deliver the mirror. Don't believe me? Come give her a scratch. You'll get a flash of what she'll do to him, and she'll get some lovies. It's a win all around."

Cerberus lowering her heads was the only kindness she would show as her snouts curled into menacing snarls.

"I'll take your word for it," I spat at his rather effective intimidation tactic.

"Thank you, my sweet." Patting Cerberus on the side, Hades jerked his head in the direction from which she had come. "You're free to go, while Alastor and I finish our chat."

A reluctant snort, and Cerberus turned in a wide circle to make her retreat.

"So, you see," Hades made a grand display of throwing his arms out wide, "you can believe me, or don't. Check with the mirror, or don't. It really makes no difference to me, either way. My only stipulation is that, when the time comes, you give the mirror to Amphrite. Elsewise, newly acquired scars will *pale* in comparison to the torture inflicted on your colorful little friend."

A roll of blue flame, and the Lord of the Underworld ... vanished.

CHAPTER TWENTY THREE

He was known as one of the most admirable and kind royals Atlantica had ever been blessed with," I muttered into the silence left in Hades' wake. Turning to Sterling, I blinked hard in my search for understanding. "Now, look at what he's become. A monster willing to kill and manipulate to claim his vengeance."

"In the name of those he cared for." After coming to in a heap, Sterling found an aloe leaf moist with dew to treat his wounds. Snapping it in half, he gently pressed it to the puffed blue lines marring his face, wincing at the first touch. "Many have done far worse for love. Not that it justifies cruelty."

"You okay?" I asked, jerking my chin at the wounds he gingerly tended to.

"I will be. I wager it looks worse than it feels." A slathering of nature's healing applied, he cast the broken leaf aside.

The vivid stripes had faded to faint shadows. Even so, that didn't change the fact that Hades disfigured Sterling without so much as a touch. We stood no chance against that caliber of power. We were trapped, utterly at the mercy of the demi-god. Still, I had made a promise to young Phin. A stipulation required to honor the lad's sacrifice. Stare drifting to the beckoning gold frame cradled in the grass, my feet floated me closer to it under their own accord.

"I ... have to know the truth. If there is yet a way to save Queen Evelyn, we owe it to Phin and the royal family to discover it." Crouching down beside the mirror, I traced my fingers over the peaks and valleys of its elaborate frame. Careful not to shift my gaze to its surface quite yet. "I don't know what awaits within the looking glass—"

Pressing his damaged lips into a thin line, Sterling nodded his saddened understanding. "You need your peace to focus. My presence is a bit ... off-putting. I'll go, and leave you to it."

"*No!*" I yelped before he could shuffle even one step away. "Please, last time it was so real. So enveloping. I fear if the reflection draws me in too deep, I'll never find my way out again. Will you act as my tether?"

Eyes narrowed with suspicion, he considered my plea. "How would *I* do that?"

Palm raised, I showed him the stone. "Hold tight to this, pressing it into my skin to remind me of what's real. If it looks like I'm in distress, grind it to the bone if you have to."

"Such a task would require a high level of ... trust," Sterling pointed out, pushing a pebble with the toe of his boot.

Knees settling into the dirt, I spoke the truth he needed to hear. "Yes, Sterling, I *trust* you. And, I need your help. I can't do this without you. That said, I need your word you won't get distracted by butterflies, shiny objects, or your own mind. Can you swear that to me? That you're able to maintain focus?"

Narrow chest swelled with purpose, he marched to my side. Plopping down cross-legged beside me, his back stayed straight with rock-solid resolve. "No distractions," he vowed.

Gripping the top of the mirror, I tipped it toward me and found my mouth suddenly parched with fear. "Then I suppose there's no need for further delay."

Laying his hand over mine, Sterling squeezed the stone into my palm for a quick pulse. "Trust me with this charge, and know I will not fail you. It's been too long since anyone believed in me for me to take such a thing lightly."

With the gleam of the mirror's face staring back at me, my skin crawled. "My friend, my hesitation has nothing whatsoever to do with you."

"Oh," Sterling's grip eased a bit. "In that case, take your time."

I swallowed hard, trying to pry my gaze up to the reflection, and made it as far as the frame. Lingering in the swirls and gold-etched foliage, I accepted the moment for the brief reprieve it was. The calm before the storm. The pallet cleanser before the main course. The clink of the locking shackles before the lashings began...

Realizing I was purposely stalling, and making matters worse, I bit the inside of my cheek hard enough to taste the coppery rush of blood, and forced myself to face the center of the glass.

I locked stares with my reflection, and felt a tug from within. A pull on the line, reeling me closer. Before I could blink, an energy seized hold and dragged me under. Sterling's screams fading behind me, I fell victim to the mirror's unyielding demand.

Thrust into the howling abyss within the looking glass, the unrelenting hold of my faithful tether was all that prevented me from being swallowed whole. A sea of truth raged all around, slamming me from all sides with more than I ever wanted to know.

A baby born.
A tapestry torn.
A curse invoked.
A prince croaked.
An apple bit.
A perfect fit.
A magic kiss.
Ever after bliss.
A heart stolen.
Heads a rollin'.
A spinning wheel.
A yearning to be real.

So many stories, ebbing and flowing in the ceaseless current of life. I felt every torturous horror inflicted on Vanessa. Watched Sterling's spiral into madness. Heard the crunch of Evelyn's bones as the life was squeezed from her. Learned the deadly secrets of those anointed as gods, and what they would do to anyone that discovered them. Knew how everything would play out until the end of days, and the significance each thread of life held in the intricate tapestry of fate. All of these answers—to questions I never wished to ask—were splayed out before me.

Anguished wail swelling in my chest, I screamed my throat raw into the void. Nothing touched me. Nothing had to. Millions of shallow cuts of truth sliced away who I was, and all that I believed. That pain scarred far deeper than any flaying of flesh.

Breakers of knowledge pounded the fight out of me. Falling slack, my fingers slipped from Sterling's hand. I resigned myself to let go, if only to make the hurt stop.

The lad on the other side of the glass, however, was not prepared or willing to lose me without a fight. Jerking my arm with a force that threatened to dislocate my shoulder, Sterling wrenched me from the mirror with a deafening roar.

It would be a vast understatement to say I came out of the mirror a different man than the one that went in. Jaded by how the play would unfold before the first line was uttered.

Falling to my hands and knees, I struggled to catch my breath. Damp hair clung to my skin, sweat streaking down my back. "Thank you," I panted.

"No thanks are required. I'm simply glad I had the strength to pull you out. What did you see?" Sterling asked, his tone cautiously apprehensive.

A maniacal laugh bubbled up my throat at the mere thought of where I would begin. The harsh mallet of reality pounded down a choked sob before it could seep from my lips. Searching the lifetimes of information that ravaged me, I fought for the memory of what it was I had been looking for. I fell forward, my forehead in the dirt, and let my head loll in Sterling's direction.

"The queen?" he helpfully offered. "Can she be saved?"

Pushing off the ground, I dragged my palms over my grime-covered face. "Old magics were used to snuff the life from the fair queen. Had they not, the sickness blackening Evelyn's innards would have claimed her by week's end. There was nothing we could have done, from the moment we entered that kingdom, to save her. Now, another wears the face of Caselotti's queen." The clip of my words reflected no emotion, only harsh fact.

Slumping back with his rump on his heels, Sterling hung his head. "So, that's it then. Our only option is to give the mirror to Amphrite as Hades commands."

"It's far from the *only* one," I rasped.

Rolling on to my hip, I tucked one leg under me and let my forearm dangle over my shin. While my mind ticked through every possible route we could take and where it would land us, I noticed the sorrow behind Sterling's eyes. I had borne witness to it many times before, but only now understood the twisted roots beneath it.

"You will see Alice again," I promised. Watching his face brighten, the knowledge of the circumstances of said encounter gutted me. He couldn't know the truth. The cost was too high. Instead, I battled to keep my expression a placid neutral. "Just as I will be reunited with Vanessa. We will find them, Sterling, I promise you that. Shortly after handing over the mirror."

Chin quivering, Sterling's jade eyes swam with tears. "I can make no such guarantee, sir. The shift of time and space between jumps makes it nearly impossible to—"

I reached over and clamped his hand with mine, the bite of my infliction a nonissue. No new vision could hurt me, I had seen them all. Catching his stare, I held firm. "What hindered you in the past soon will not be a concern. Of that, you have my word, as long as you trust me. Can you do that?"

Blinking back the grips of emotion, Sterling bobbed his head in resolute confirmation. "It's been years since I've said this of another soul. But, yes, I put my faith in you, my friend."

Inhaling a lungful of purpose, I pushed from the ground and fixed my gaze on the castle looming in the distance. "You will jump us to the private quarters of King Liam. I will handle the rest."

"*You know of my concerns jumping!*" Sterling bolted to his feet, panic bulging the tendons of his neck. "I can't control it. It's not in jest when I warn of us ending up with two asses!"

Armed with the knowledge of the exact outcome, I found myself paralyzed to do more than blink in his direction. "That was before you were gifted the essence of the Menehune. It won't be long before you find yourself able to harness your affliction like never before and steer it where *you* see fit. I simply ask, before you surf off after your heart's desire, that you help me finish what we started in this realm."

"Then, you'll help me find Alice?" he asked, chewing on his lower lip.

"Then, you won't need *my* help in the least to find her," I corrected. Balling my fist, I swung back and connected with a corner of the mirror. A lone shard, barely bigger than an oak leaf, popped free from the frame. Scooping it from the ground, I offered it to him. "Consider this my vow. Keep it with you as a reminder of what you did for me, and all I owe you in return."

"You owe me nothing. We will finish this, together." Accepting the shard with one hand, the other clamped onto my wrist. As the dizzying blur of distorted motion began, I grabbed hold of the frame of the mirror to ensure it made the journey with us. We steadied in the parlor of the king's private quarters. The beginning of the end … aglow in a *beautiful* blaze.

CHAPTER TWENTY FOUR

he king woke with a start, which was not surprising
considering his curtains were on fire and smoke was filling the
room.

"Wha ... what's happening?" he murmured, rolling on to his
side. "Alastor? You're back! Does that mean you've found a— *Good
heavens! Fire! There's a fire!*"

Crouching beside the bed, I found myself unable to match his
level, or any, agitation. "Yes, there is. It will be easily contained by
the efficiency of your guards, as long as you get out of the castle
quickly."

"D-did you start it?" Clutching his blankets to his chest, King
Liam scooted up against his headboard and eyed my measured
reaction with suspicion.

"Of course not!" Sterling scoffed, from the security of his
position by the door. A beat, and his brow pinched. "Wait ... *did*
you?"

"You know I didn't. I was with *you*," I clarified. Flames
crawling farther up the wall, I pushed off the floor to perch on the
edge of the king's royal mattress. "A candle from your candelabra
tipped over, catching the bottom hem of the curtain fabric. While
the entire ordeal was completely accidental, there are those that

would use this opportunity for self-gain if we allow them the chance. We are not going to do that."

"We have to go!" Eyes widening enough to reflect the red and orange tendrils stretching skyward, Liam looked as though he wanted to bolt for the exit, yet unease prevented him from making a move to push past me.

"And we will, as soon as you understand exactly what you have to do. For the safety of your daughter, and your kingdom, you need to follow my instructions to the letter. Do you understand me?" The temperature of the room had increased by no less than thirty degrees, yet not a drop of sweat bloomed anywhere on my person. If I didn't know better, I would think it was my reflection that came out of the mirror, and not the man of flesh and bone. But that was the rub, wasn't it? I did know better. Down to specific detail.

"Yes!" the king yelped, scooting farther from the growing blaze. "Please, just hurry!"

"Happily." Hands folded in my lap, I tilted my head to the task. "As soon as I am done speaking, you're going to leave this room and run to your daughter. Alert no one. Collect the child quickly and quietly, then leave the castle at once. When you reach the gate, have the guards stationed there sound the call."

"My wife?" Liam coughed, struggling to breathe around the billowing smoke.

"Time being of the essence, that woman that insisted on sleeping in the tower is not your wife. You've known that since you watched her shun your child, and fail to lean into your touch as she always did when you ran your finger across her shoulder blade. The imposter is responsible for the death of the *real* Evelyn. You'll find her in a shallow grave at coordinates nineteen-point eight north, by one fifty-five-point eight west." Rising to my feet, I took a step back to allow him a clear path to the door. "Now, go."

King Liam needed no second invitation. Scrambling off the bed, he covered his nose and mouth with the crook of his elbow and ran for the door.

"Oh, there is one more thing," I called after him. Sterling stepped in front of the door to block the exit. "For the sake of your daughter, don't marry again."

Tears welling in his eyes, the king's face crumbled as he spoke the plea of his breaking heart. "A girl needs a mother."

"We're done with the logic portion of this conversation, then?" I asked, feigning interest. "Very well. Off you go." A nod to Sterling, and he allowed the hacking royal by.

Sauntering to the door, I watched the king disappear into his daughter's room. He emerged moments later with Snow bundled in his arms. Without a glance in our direction, his whispered steps faded down the hall.

Hungry flames claiming the room behind us, Sterling and I trailed after him in silence. Our footsteps on the marble stairs echoed off the walls of the grand foyer, thudding all around like a pulse.

At the base of the stairs, Sterling stopped and placed a finger to his lips. "Shh ... listen."

A shout in the distance.

A trumpet's blast.

And ... the castle came to life.

Screams, shouts, pounding footfalls. Most running for the doors, a few brave souls hanging behind to battle the flames.

"Shall we go search for the pseudo queen?" Calmer than I had ever seen him, Sterling hugged the mirror to his chest.

"No need," I murmured, shifting my attention in the direction of the tallest tower. "She's coming to us."

Holding a crimson robe embellished with gold silk roses closed over her flowing nightgown, the faux Evelyn sprinted down the hall. I had to give her credit, she played the part of the frantic wife and mother well. Down to shrieking for those she supposedly cared for, as her bare feet padded down the stairs. *Liam? Snow? Oh, Alastor! Thank Olympus! What's happening? Where's my family?*

Blinking in her direction, I offered no answer at first. So lost was I in searching her face for signs of the truth as I now knew it. "Where, indeed," I managed.

"We give Amphrite the mirror, then we are free," Sterling uttered the confirmation to himself, then jabbed the ornate artifact in her direction.

Rocking back on my heels, my mouth parted with a pop. "Except … that's not Amphrite."

Flawless brow puckering, faux Evelyn shook her head. "What are you talking about? You know me. You know who I am, now I demand you tell me where my child is, at once!"

Pounding footsteps overhead, and more water was rushed to king's quarters to tame the blaze.

Pausing to give them a moment to subside, I paced a slow circle around the pseudo queen. "They pray to you quite often here, and you're never shy to gift them your blessing. But, when the High Priestess beseeched you to call forth the oracle and the Trickster you were intrigued. You simply couldn't resist the urge to take a peek and see what your subjects were up to. And what did you find? Your husband manipulating humans in attempt to seek vengeance for his *past love*. How that must have stung." Halting in front of her, I showed the due respect by dipping into a deep bow. "Goddess Persephone, *Queen of the Underworld*."

Her lips parted, as if to argue. Thinking better of it, she rolled her fingers in front of her face. A twinkling spray of light and the so-called garden nymph that aided us in the courtyard stood before us in all her innocent enchantment.

Jerking back, Sterling nearly lost hold of the mirror and scrambled for a better hold. "Give the mirror to Amphrite, then we are free," he reiterated in growing confusion.

Pursing her full, cherry lips, she cast a mock pout in Sterling's direction. "Poor child. As if your reality isn't skewed enough."

"I … called to you," Sterling stammered, struggling to catch up.

"Many do." Batting her lashes, Persephone clasped her hands over her heart.

Legs threatening to fail him, Sterling stumbled back a step. "You said things that spoke to the hearts of *many*."

"Oh, that," she giggled with a dramatic roll of her moss green eyes. "I have, like, three or four go-to things I say to all mortals. I've found no matter what their lot in life is, they find *something* in it that resonates with them. Let's see, there's; *if you act in darkness, you're no better than those that hurt you, this won't bring him or her back, he had no one before you,* and … my favorite … *it's time to start believing in yourself.* I considered those, along with my sheer presence, to be my little way of helping those in need."

"Is that what you call what you did for Queen Evelyn?" I pressed, leveling her with a glare. "Helping her?"

"Alastor, don't let this world darken your fair heart." Her pert face folded in mock sorrow. "She was suffering. I ended her pain and gave her to the earth. Beautiful flowers will bloom in her memory. That's what I do, I'm the goddess of renewed life through boundless flora."

"Then, you commandeered her identity to manipulate your husband, and us," I added, growing bored with her incessant string of lies.

Darkness sharpened the goddess' features with a deadly edge, slashing away her virtuous façade. "He detected a malevolent female energy here and *assumed* it to be Amphrite? Prophet, *please*. I was forming the River Styx while she was still growing into her sea shell bra."

"Do you claim to love him? Is that the motivation driving this little snit?" I watched the cut of my words lash against her with a triumphant rush. Her skin rippled with a thick tree-trunk hide. Barbs of thorns rose from her shoulders before she could shake off their effects.

"Love is a vicious master to those weak of heart. I seek honor, and that is where my darling *husband* has failed miserably." Tossing her cascade of flaxen hair over her shoulder, she fought her way back to her beguiling disguise. "Olympus is accustomed to its fair share of scandals. Seems not a day goes by that Zeus isn't bestowing his ... ahem, *godliness* on someone, or something. Even so, none among us were prepared for the backlash of Hades bedding Poseidon's queen. Zeus viewed he and his brothers as a holy trinity, and was furious to have their bond threatened in any way. Hades asking to be reassigned gave ole Lightning for Brains a chance to remind him of who held the power amongst them. Moving him to the Underworld *should* have been enough. A lesson learned in the deepest pits of hell. But no. I was *gifted* to him. Torn from the world above where I planted seeds, blessed farms, and awoke the sleeping plants in spring, I was forced to the Underworld as Hades' bride. Still, I wasn't *her*—his dearly departed Titonis—therefore he wouldn't even look at me. Shunned by my husband, I was alone, and stranded in a writhing pit of anguished souls. Arranged marriage or not, for *that*, I will never forgive him."

Sterling held the mirror out in front of him, seeking answers from his own bewildered reflection. "Give the mirror to Amphrite…"

Filling her lungs, Persephone jabbed her index finger in Sterling's direction. "Fix your boy before I do."

"With pleasure." I threw my arms out wide in a grand gesture. "Shall I go back a tad farther to give him a bit of backstory?"

Eyes narrowing with challenge, the goddess dragged the tip of her tongue over her top teeth. "By all means, *astound* me." Before I could begin, she turned on the ball of her foot and strode to the stairs with her head held high. With great flourish she arranged herself cross-legged on them, as if they were a bejeweled throne.

Easing the mirror from Sterling's white-knuckled grip, I lowered it gently to the floor. "Magic demands a counterbalance," I began, "as it did with you and I. Do you remember what I told you about Vanessa? How she evoked a spell that banished Amphrite from the sea and her newborn child?"

Sterling's head bobbed in an uneasy confirmation.

"The necessary balance to that incantation is what landed Amphrite right where she could be the most detrimental to Vanessa's future. In this case, that was the garden of Persephone." Hearing the goddess gasp at my revelation, I refused to let up. Let her choke on the truth. "The moment she learned who Amphrite was, the goddess welcomed her into the folds of her protection. Not out of kindness, but that she may use her to get back at Hades. Even now, as she sits there watching us, she has Poseidon's widow tucked away somewhere for safe keeping."

"Amphrite was never here? Am *I*?" I could see Sterling slipping, his hold on reality crumbling to sand in his grasp.

My only chance to reel him back was to talk fast and get to the point. "You are, my friend. And you're clever enough to see that demi-gods aren't clairvoyant. There's much they don't know. Hades has no clue his wife is in this realm. And Persephone? She fails to grasp the depths of her husband's rage when it comes to that particular ex-mermaid. You see, he believes Amphrite is here in this room right now, and can't bring himself to stay away despite his diligent planning."

Out of the corner of my eye, I watched Persephone bristle and fought to suppress a victorious grin.

Finding himself able to follow along, Sterling perked. "Meaning?"

"Any minute now we are going to find ourselves caught between warring gods."

Scarred jaws sinking into a frown, Sterling sagged. "That seems like something you could have mentioned *before* we made this trip."

CHAPTER TWENTY FIVE

Persephone leapt to her feet, looking more goddess of war than vegetation. "Hades is coming *here*? Now?"

"*Mhm*." I confirmed with a nonchalant nod.

Bringing her hands together as if in prayer, Persephone pressed the tips of her fingers to her lips. Her gaze worked side to side; feverishly scheming and plotting. "This is good. Splendid, in fact. We can have it out right here, in a *long* overdue summit of violent diplomacy."

"That's one way to play it." Letting one shoulder rise and fall, I sauntered to the stairs and sagged against the rail. "Or, you could keep the upper hand you've been so clever to earn."

"How so?" she pressed, eyes narrowing to slits.

"He believes Amphrite wants the mirror—"

"Give the mirror to Amphrite," Sterling interrupted, unfortunately still stuck on his loop.

Casting my stare to the slate floor, I let him finish before pushing on. "Even if she were, she would have no need for it. There is a far more powerful tool here."

Bristling with the suspicion I was toying with her, Persephone dropped her hands to her sides and rolled her shoulders into a haughty posture. "And what, pray tell, would that be? You? Is this some pathetic plea for your life? Because, I think I can save you some time; I only want the mirror. Hades deems it important, and I want to know why. You two, on the other hand, hold no such value or appeal to me. Therefore, I fully intend to recycle you into fertilizer for my daylilies. They've been looking a bit drab as of late."

"I make no such plea for mercy, Your Highness. I know the humble part I play, all too well. I actually was speaking of my friend, here." Glancing up from under my brow, I watched Sterling blanch under the scrutiny of the spotlight forced upon him. "The mirror gives answers, nothing more. Hades and the king were both so fixated on that, they ignored a far more valuable treasure. Imagine being able to travel anywhere, in any realm, with the power of a passing thought. A fortune telling parlor trick pales in comparison to such a pearl, does it not? Unbind Sterling's full potential, and he could be the chariot to your heart's desire. Just think of all the devilish ways you could concoct to torment Hades armed with such a weapon."

Hands on her hips, Persephone glared down the bridge of her nose in Sterling's direction. "Is this true? Do you have such a talent?"

Mouth opening and closing in search of his place in this farce, Sterling could manage only a nod.

Persephone wet her lips, circling him in a predatory swagger. "Why would you tell me such a thing? What's in it for you?"

"Alastor, what's happening?" Chest rising and falling, Sterling twitched with fear.

"What's in it for me? Freedom from a life I simply don't fit in." Raising my hand before me, I pantomimed picking at my cuticles. It was a pointless act I used only to spare myself the guilt of seeing the pain and confusion etched into Sterling's features. "He and I are bonded, you see. Sever that tie, and his abilities will be limitless."

"Y-you said it couldn't be d-done," Sterling stammered, voice breaking as the dull blade of betrayal ground deep. "That we were in this together."

"What can I say? You really should have considered all the *pieces*," my pointed gaze lobbed from his face, to the shard of glass stowed away in his coin purse, and back again, "before believing such a thing."

"So, that's what this is about?" Persephone groaned her exasperated annoyance. "Some mortal desire to return home? You are all so tediously predictable."

"Something like that," I admitted with a sad smile.

Throwing her hands up in growing disinterest, the goddess played along. "Tell me of this bond then, and how I sever it?"

"First, I need your word no harm will come to him, or any that I love. Including Hades' own daughter, Princess Vanessa. I wager Amphrite will contest greatly to that. Oh, and one final stipulation. The mirror gets left behind, all except that missing shard, of course." Stare locked with Sterling's, I watched the cloak of realization set in. His fingers wandered into the folds of his drawstring purse. "That will be a brilliant way to throw Hades off your trail."

"Controlling Amphrite will *not* be an issue. Chain someone to a wall far enough away, and they become quite the un-encumbering houseguest." Drumming her fingers together, she chewed on the offer. "I *do* like the idea of having more time to cook up something perfectly devious for my sorry excuse for a husband. Very well, I will agree to your terms, *only* if your friend can help me secure a lasting and final vengeance against Hades. I'm talking something diabolically twisted."

"He's been tortured, imprisoned, and enslaved. Not that he likes to speak of such unpleasantries. I'm sure he can help you come up with just the thing. Can't you, Sterling?" My pleading stare beseeched him, begging for him to understand that I was fighting to protect him in the only way I knew how. In order for him to be spared, I had to paint him as the most vital element in this portrait of revenge. Elsewise, his ravings would have him killed before nightfall. The mirror showed me the brutal nature of his death. I had no intention of allowing him to become victim to such depraved cruelty.

Perplexed, yet compliant, he dutifully nodded.

Another piece arranged. Still, it wasn't enough. The knowledge within the looking glass still had to be protected. That job fell to me alone.

"Then, we have an accord?" Eyebrows raised in question, Persephone offered me her hand.

Fingers closing around hers, I lowered my head in a bow of respect. "That we do, my Queen."

"Fantastic." Snatching her hand away as if worried I would contaminate her with humanity, her nose crinkled with a distaste she no longer attempted to hide. "Let us then discuss this tie that must be broken."

I steeled myself for what was to come, offered her a tight smile, and walked to Sterling with my slow, measured steps clicking through the cavernous foyer. "I discovered the truth when I ventured into the mirror. Surrounded by knowledge of pain, famine, and ... *war*," a subtle glance in Persephone's direction hinted at the cataclysmic conflict brewing between the gods, "I thought it to be your hand that was holding me back from spiraling into that abyss. But, I was wrong. It's nothing as weak as flesh. It's a connection in our spirits that prevents us from losing ourselves to these inflictions forced upon us. To sever that bond ... one must die."

Head thrown back in a throaty guffaw, Persephone clapped with delight. "A voluntary sacrifice? And it's not even my birthday!"

The shard held tight in his hand, Sterling gaped down at it in horror. "No! I couldn't possibly! There has to be another way!"

Edging in closer, my voice dropped to a soothing whisper. "There isn't, my friend, but it's okay. With this, you'll finally be able to get back to Alice. All you suffered through, everything you've endured, won't be for naught."

"You're a hero. What am I?" Sterling tried to drop his arm to his side.

Catching his elbow, I kept the shard pointed out. I positioned myself at its tip, feeling the pressure in the tender tissue between my ribs and leaned into it. "*You* are a soul untarnishable by the ugliness of this world. One purer of heart than I could ever hope to be. For too long you've felt unworthy of home or family." Arms wrapped around him, I pressed into that deadly embrace — accepting the blinding bite of pain for the temporary affliction it was. Against his ear, I murmured, "This ... is my way of freeing you, my brother. Go, find your way back to the love you deserve."

Ribbons of crimson unfolded from my gut as I sagged against him. Shoulders shaking with sobs, he lowered me to the floor as gently as he could. "Alastor, what have you done? What about Vanessa?"

Chin quaking with the chill of blood loss, I offered him a waning smile. "This … is the only way … we can both … go … home." My eyes wanted to shut, the pull of the current washing me onward. "Keep … the shard … with you."

Unable and unwilling to fight that demanding tide, I gave in and let it toss and churn what was left of me into the confines of the mirror.

CHAPTER TWENTY SIX

*E*ngland, 1865.

Buggies puttered over cobblestone streets. The men driving extended a friendly wave or tip of the hat to those they passed. Women and girls in full skirts folded their hands in a demure fashion, and scurried off for afternoon tea.

In the backyard of one regal estate, a young man with a distorted smile riffled through clothes hung on a line.

"What is this place, and how is it going to help me ensure Hades' eternal suffering?" Persephone sneered, recoiling at a tabby cat that rubbed against her ankle.

"This is where we are going to find Alice and heal her." Sterling paused in his task to pat his satchel where the key to her cure was safely stowed away.

Shoulders rising to her ears with equal parts rage and disgust, the goddess' face reddened. "I don't care about any Alice!"

Face falling slack of emotion, he blinked in her direction. "Oh, but you should. Legend states that she's the only one who can defeat the Jabberwock."

"What, in Olympus' name, is a Jabberwock?" she erupted, crossing the line into foot-stomping annoyance.

"I don't know. What's a Jabberwock?" he lobbed back.

Persephone's mouth swung open, words momentarily locked on her tongue. "What? I don't know. You said it!"

"No, I didn't," he argued and returned to his task. "And, that was a most terrible riddle. Really, you're capable of much better."

"I didn't — Ugh!" Throwing her hands in the air, the Queen of the Underworld paced a circle around the meticulously clipped yard. "Can you at least tell me where we are?"

Unclipping a few items from the line, Sterling tossed the wardrobe change at her. "We will discover that soon enough. If I could offer a suggestion, though? All the worlds I have traveled in, for some reason layers translate to wisdom. I don't understand the logic, but the more I bundle the more respect and kindness I'm shown."

Pinching the corner of his change purse, Sterling peered down at the shard of glass tucked safely within and offered it a knowing wink.

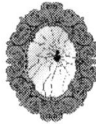

"Mirror, mirror, on the wall. I order you, now, to answer my call."

Turning away from my link to Sterling's reality, I drifted on a surge of knowledge to face out of the looking glass. My essence — all that remained of me — resided within that endless void. As the oracle, it fell to me to protect the mirror from being wielded for unthinkable evil and destruction. Now, I controlled what information would be revealed, and to whom. Sacrificing myself had been a noble necessity. Yet, I couldn't have fathomed the toll it would take. On Marooner's Rock, Phin asked me to send him any lost boys. When one is lost, there is hope. Hope of finding family, a home, or even one's self. Where I was stretched beyond the reaches of all hope or optimism. I was … gone.

Gazing out at the catacomb caves of the Underworld, I met Hades' intense glower with disinterested obedience. "You called, my liege?"

Hand curled around the edge of the frame, Hades chewed on the inside of his cheek. The screams of tortured souls wailed in the distance, echoing through the cavernous hollow. "Someone is protecting Amphrite from me. And *you* know who it is. Perhaps uncovering that knowledge is how you found yourself … entombed in glass." His attention roamed over the sea of emptiness surrounding me. "Regardless, you swore allegiance to me. I, alone, can offer you freedom from your prison in the sweet release of death. But that is a tender morsel you earn only by helping me destroy those that *dare* stand against me. What say you, *slave*?"

Glaring up at him from under my brow, I spat the words with murderous hatred, "How may I serve you ... my master?"

CHAPTER TWENTY SEVEN

Within the glass, I saw a war.

A clashing of gods scratched at the door.

Left unchecked, they would've choked life from the world.

Their cloak of annihilation violently unfurled.

Mortals were used as their unwilling pawns,

Oblivious to the darkness that would snuff out the dawn.

Along the way, I became a pupil.

Manipulating influence by targeting their scruples.

Careful positioning is required for their inevitable battle,

To save the realm from becoming scorched and charred chattel.

Entombed in glass, I find myself cursed,

To prevent the enraged gods from doing their worst.

I count the seconds 'til this mirror shatters in a magnificent spray,

Allowing me to hold Vanessa one glorious day.

Knowing exactly when, and the stipulations of how,

Grants me the wisdom to make this solemn vow;

Lord and Lady of the Underworld, soon it will be your turn.

When I'm free from this tomb ... I'll watch you both burn.

ROURKE

The Unfortunate Soul Chronicles continue with

Pursuing Madness

Venture too far and lose who you are...

Coming Soon!

About the Author

Stacey Rourke is the award-winning author of works that span genres. She lives in Michigan with her husband, two beautiful daughters, and two giant dogs. She loves to travel, has an unhealthy shoe addiction, and considers herself blessed to make a career out of talking to the imaginary people that live in her head.

Connect with her at:

www.staceyrourke.com
Facebook at www.facebook.com/staceyrourkeauthor
Amazon Author Page: http://amzn.to/2l8FlbH
or on Twitter or instagram @rourkewrites

If you enjoyed The Unfortunate Soul Chronicles, pick up these other titles by Stacey Rourke:

The Gryphon Series

The Conduit
Embrace
Sacrifice
Ascension
Descent
Inferno
Coming Soon: Revelation

The Legends Saga

Crane
Raven
Steam

Reel Romance

Adapted for Film
Turn Tables

TS901 CHRONICLES

Co-written with Tish Thawer
TS901: Anomaly
Coming Soon: TS901: Dominion

Veiled Series

Veiled
Coming Soon: Vlad

Printed in Great Britain
by Amazon